"Ever felt that your job is the equivalent of a theme-park exhibit? *Pastoralia* will not refute such subversive notions, but it makes them tolerably, screamingly funny."
—*Time*

"Savage, soulful satires . . . It always feels like a global environmental catastrophe or a horrible nuclear accident is just offstage in Saunders's grimly satirical, neo-futurist stories—even if they're about something as simple as the aftermath of a self-help seminar or a boy on his bicycle. Nevertheless, Saunders is also a tremendously funny writer. Like all great humorists, he understands and mines the close kinship of the horse laugh and the morbid shudder. A master of distilling the disorders of our time into fiction, Saunders also has the good sense to reach for literary truths that transcend the moment. And for that very reason, we should savor the witty, arch, and quietly redemptive tales of *Pastoralia*: George Saunders is a better writer than the moment deserves."
—*Salon*

"Taut, witty, disturbing . . . derivative of nobody. [*Pastoralia's*] stories are every bit as finely tuned, mordantly funny, and original as those in *CivilWarLand in Bad Decline*."
—*The Atlantic Monthly*

"A short-story collection reminiscent of T. Coraghessan Boyle . . . and Thomas Pynchon. Saunders has concocted a satirically sadistic metaphor for how too many Americans see their lives. A classic of workplace paranoia for whose equal one would have to go back to Joseph Heller. . . . Bitterly uproarious . . . [as] funny as hell."
—*San Francisco Chronicle*

"Bizarre and original stories . . . freakish and lovely. It [looks] as if Saunders has forged a one-man genre; call it Theme Park Surrealism."
—*LA Weekly*

"Not since Ignatius J. Reilly and company in John Kennedy Toole's *A Confederacy of Dunces* has there been a band of dunderheads so delightful . . . [and] so strange that one must resort to a cliche to describe them: You really *won't* know whether to laugh or cry."
—*Kansas City Star*

"Sharp satirical stories . . . [Saunders's] skewed portraits of American life somehow retain a marvelous humanity. Even bizarre twists like a decomposing relative who returns from the grave to torture her family are weighted with a sadness that, as in life, mitigates the absurdist elements. [A] brutal . . . hilarious, strange, clear-eyed look at the twenty-first century."
—*US Weekly*

"Damnable characters and twisted plot lines parade through the pages of *Pastoralia*, [confirming] Saunders's skills as a humorist, an imaginative sadist, and a literary craftsman. . . . He dares the unexpected . . . [and] shines a new light on the art of the tale." —*Minneapolis Star Tribune*

"Like Flannery O'Connor and Nathanael West, Saunders knows that you can mine the banal for humor. Close to miraculous . . . utterly wonderful." —*The Austin Chronicle*

"Stories so precisely rendered and wildly creative, these worlds become favorite places to return to. Saunders's prose is like drug candy, compulsively swallowed, sweetly addictive . . . anarchic and startling." —*San Francisco Bay Guardian*

"To discover George Saunders is to stumble into a world you never knew existed, like Alice's Wonderland. In *Pastoralia*, his arresting originality, deadpan delivery, and satiric vision of contemporary America secure his place as the bold successor to Thomas Pynchon and Kurt Vonnegut. Saunders takes our basest fears and reflects them back to us." —*Nylon*

PRAISE FOR
CIVILWARLAND IN BAD DECLINE
A *NEW YORK TIMES* NOTABLE BOOK
ONE OF *ENTERTAINMENT WEEKLY*'S
TEN BEST FICTION BOOKS OF 2000

"The debut of an exciting new voice in fiction. Mr. Saunders writes like the illegitimate offspring of [Nathanael] West and Kurt Vonnegut, perhaps a distant relative of Mark Leyner and Steven Wright. He's a savage satirist with a sentimental streak who delineates, in these pages, the dark underbelly of the American dream: the losses, delusions, and terrors suffered by the lonely, the disenfranchised, the downtrodden, and the plain unlucky. . . . Bizarre events pop up regularly in *CivilWarLand* like road signs on a highway, directing the reader toward the dark heart of Mr. Saunders's America. What powers the stories along is Mr. Saunders's wonderfully demented language, his ear for absurdity and slang, his own patented blend of psychobabble, techno-talk, and existential angst. Mr. Saunders's satiric vision of America is dark and demented; it is also ferocious and very funny." —Michiko Kakutani, *The New York Times*

continued . . .

"An astoundingly tuned voice—graceful, dark, authentic, and funny—telling just the kinds of stories we need to get us through these times."
                                                                    —Thomas Pynchon

"Ingenious . . . full of savage humor and originality [and] scorching brilliance . . . The author creates a nightmarish post-apocalyptic world that might have been envisioned by Walt Disney on acid. Having visited the claustrophobic landscapes of Saunders's fiction, it's hard to view a strip mall or an amusement park the same way again. His perspective on the everyday American apocalypse leaves us chilled, but also gives us the satisfaction of identifying with his beleaguered heroes who maintain their integrity against formidable odds. . . . In *CivilWarLand in Bad Decline*, George Saunders is improvising around a single scary note. Few writers have sounded it with such clarity, boldness, and wit."
                                                                    —*The Philadelphia Inquirer*

"The dystopian short story is alive and kicking, wearing a black leather jacket—maybe stolen in a barroom brawl—and telling deadly dark, off-color jokes. His name is George Saunders, and he's half-huckster, half-saint; he's got shades of both Denis Johnson and Raymond Chandler. . . . Twisted and heartbreaking at once . . . so intense that it borders on dementia. The world he delivers is a near-tomorrow of plagues and starvation, genetic purity and cyber-terrorism, but it's also treacherously funny. The future envisioned in *CivilWarLand* may be improbable, but its imagined horrors have a queasy familiarity, as if you've been there before in the worst of your dreams. . . . By turns he's ferocious, witty, and uproarious, but what makes his fiction memorable is the gravitas of its dark portraiture of America."
                                                                    —*The Boston Globe*

"Alarming [and] funny . . . More satirist than futurist, Saunders invites comparison less to Aldous Huxley than to Kurt Vonnegut. . . . He has a touching habit of bringing to fullness the kind of people who are regularly marginalized. . . . This is George Saunders's first book, and it is the debut of an original, darkly funny voice from whom we can hope to hear more."
                                                                    —*The Atlanta Journal-Constitution*

"Scary, hilarious, and unforgettable . . . George Saunders is a writer of arresting brilliance and originality."
                                                                    —Tobias Wolff

"One hopes Mr. Saunders is not exactly a visionary. Yet he is demonstrably a cool satirist and a wicked stylist. *CivilWarLand in Bad Decline* is just about the quirkiest and most accomplished short-story debut since Barry Hannah's *Airships*. Mr. Saunders has an ear for the offbeat cadences of the contemporary idiom, not least the language of businessmen. . . . His stories take surprising and sometimes stunning turns. Quite unexpectedly, between guffaws, you find yourself moved. Mr. Saunders is one of those rare writers who can effortlessly blend satire and sentiment."

—Jay McInerney, *The New York Times Book Review*

THE BRIEF AND FRIGHTENING REIGN OF PHIL

"Reminiscent of vintage Vonnegut with a dash of Dr. Seuss, this tale of an absurdist border war captures the aggrieved jingoism of Bush's America without ever preaching."   —*Details* (#1 Fall Read)

"Fascinating . . . Darkly funny, deeply human . . . *Phil* is the illustrated tale of two countries full of strange creatures, and what happens when one country gets taken over by a warmongering tyrant named Phil."

—*Entertainment Weekly*

"The book is a riff—and a very amusing one, I hasten to add—on any number of twentieth-century monstrosities. . . . Madly inventive."

—*The Boston Globe*

"Many critics refer to Saunders as a satirist, and though the term is often used in conjunction with names like Swift and Twain, it can also be a trap. The world a satirist creates, some charge, is only a prediction or, at best, a distortion, as though all successful art isn't about distorting, or bending, reality. Another word that gets fastened to Saunders is *moralist*. These two terms are often intertwined, of course. At the core of much satire is some kind of prescription. Still, even if correct, these two labels, the limitations of the first and the taint of the scold in the second, don't do justice to Saunders. His bleak but merciful stories contain a great deal more than satire, or at least the toothless send-ups that often stand in for satire, and they are never preachy. . . . The message of *The Brief and Frightening Reign of Phil*, delivered with great wit, isn't overtly political . . . but there is no denying the noble rage at the heart of this book. . . . Stunning . . . Brilliant."   —Sam Lipsyte, *Bookforum*

continued . . .

"Extraordinary . . . Saunders's fable of imperialism and exceptionalism is some parts Orwellian caustic vision, some parts shaded Dr. Seuss whimsy, some parts Pynchonian satire but mostly Saunders's own original, bemused take on the world as he finds it."   —*The Morning News*

"*The Brief and Frightening Reign of Phil* is a political fable of a world unbound from the physical laws of our own, but not so unlike it for all that. . . . One of the many pleasures of this little book is the sheer physical weirdness of Saunders's characters; take Phil's flirting techniques, which involve 'inflating and deflating his central bladder in order to look more manly and attractive.' Saunders also has a perfect ear for political rhetoric, and so we get the National Life Enjoyment Index Score, the Certificate of Total Approval (signed by Phil's cronies), and the Peace Encouraging Enclosure (a jail, of course). *Phil* is more than a send-up of the machinations of power than a direct satire of our country . . . but it doesn't feel so unfamiliar, either."   —*Esquire*

"Like George Orwell's *Animal Farm*, Saunders finds a backdoor into our conscience through surrealism, albeit of a more ironic stripe. . . . So many real-world events can be seen here, but the genius of this book, however, is not its applicability, but rather how it convinces us to care for a beleaguered people—without allowing us the cozy certitude that they are us."
          —*The Newark Star-Ledger*

"In *The Brief and Frightening Reign of Phil*, Saunders has sketched a parable about the abuses of power that has an unlikely sting in its whimsy. . . . Its imagery and perverse cruelties linger in the mind after you've read it."
          —*The Seattle Times*

ALSO BY GEORGE SAUNDERS

The Very Persistent Gappers of Frip
CivilWarLand in Bad Decline
The Brief and Frightening Reign of Phil
In Persuasion Nation
The Braindead Megaphone

RIVERHEAD BOOKS

New York

PASTORALIA

· stories by ·

GEORGE SAUNDERS

RIVERHEAD BOOKS
An imprint of Penguin Random House LLC
375 Hudson Street
New York, New York 10014

All of these stories originally appeared in *The New Yorker*, in some cases in a
condensed form.

The Library of Congress has catalogued the Riverhead hardcover edition as follows:

Saunders, George.
Pastoralia : stories / by George Saunders.
    p. cm.
Contents: Pastoralia—Winky—Sea Oak—The end of FIRPO in the world—
The barber's unhappiness—The falls.
ISBN 1573221619
I. Title.
PS3569.A7897 E53 2000   99-087258
813'.54—dc21

First Riverhead hardcover edition: May 2000
First Riverhead trade paperback edition: June 2001
Riverhead trade paperback ISBN: 9781573228725

Printed in the United States of America

36th Printing

Book design by Judith Stagnitto Abbate

• *Contents* •

PASTORALIA

· PASTORALIA ·

1.

I HAVE TO ADMIT I'm not feeling my best. Not that I'm doing so bad. Not that I really have anything to complain about. Not that I would actually verbally complain if I did have something to complain about. No. Because I'm Thinking Positive/Saying Positive. I'm sitting back on my haunches, waiting for people to poke in their heads. Although it's been thirteen days since anyone poked in their head and Janet's speaking English to me more and more, which is partly why I feel so, you know, crummy.

"Jeez," she says first thing this morning. "I'm so tired of roast goat I could scream."

What am I supposed to say to that? It puts me in a bad spot. She thinks I'm a goody-goody and that her speaking English makes me uncomfortable. And she's right. It does. Because we've got it good. Every morning, a new goat, just killed, sits in our Big Slot. In our Little Slot, a book of matches. That's better than some. Some are required to catch wild hares in snares. Some are required to wear pioneer garb while cutting the heads off chickens. But not us. I just have to haul the dead goat out of the Big Slot and skin it with a sharp flint. Janet just has to make the fire. So things are pretty good. Not as good as in the old days, but then again, not so bad.

In the old days, when heads were constantly poking in, we liked what we did. Really hammed it up. Had little grunting fights. Whenever I was about to toss a handful of dirt in her face I'd pound a rock against a rock in rage. That way she knew to close her eyes. Sometimes she did this kind of crude weaving. It was like: Roots of Weaving. Sometimes we'd go down to Russian Peasant Farm for a barbecue, I remember there was Murray and Leon, Leon was dating Eileen, Eileen was the one with all the cats, but now, with the big decline in heads poking in, the Russian Peasants are all elsewhere, some to Administration but most not, Eileen's cats have gone wild, and honest to God sometimes I worry I'll go to the Big Slot and find it goatless.

2.

This morning I go to the Big Slot and find it goatless. Instead of a goat there's a note:

Hold on, hold on, it says. *The goat's coming, for crissake. Don't get all snooty.*

The problem is, what am I supposed to do during the time when I'm supposed to be skinning the goat with the flint? I decide to pretend to be desperately ill. I rock in a corner and moan. This gets old. Skinning the goat with the flint takes the better part of an hour. No way am I rocking and moaning for an hour.

Janet comes in from her Separate Area and her eyebrows go up.

"No freaking goat?" she says.

I make some guttural sounds and some motions meaning: Big rain come down, and boom, make goats run, goats now away, away in high hills, and as my fear was great, I did not follow.

Janet scratches under her armpit and makes a sound like a monkey, then lights a cigarette.

"What a bunch of shit," she says. "Why you insist, I'll never know. Who's here? Do you see anyone here but us?"

I gesture to her to put out the cigarette and make the fire. She gestures to me to kiss her butt.

"Why am I making a fire?" she says. "A fire in advance of a goat. Is this like a wishful fire? Like a hopeful fire? No, sorry, I've had it. What would I do in the real world if there was thunder and so on and our goats actually ran away? Maybe I'd mourn, like cut myself with that flint, or maybe I'd kick your ass for being so stupid as to leave the goats out in the rain. What, they didn't put it in the Big Slot?"

I scowl at her and shake my head.

"Well, did you at least check the Little Slot?" she says. "Maybe it was a small goat and they really crammed it in. Maybe for once they gave us a nice quail or something."

I give her a look, then walk off in a rolling gait to check the Little Slot.

Nothing.

"Well, freak this," she says. "I'm going to walk right out of here and see what the hell is up."

But she won't. She knows it and I know it. She sits on her log and smokes and together we wait to hear a clunk in the Big Slot.

About lunch we hit the Reserve Crackers. About dinner we again hit the Reserve Crackers.

No heads poke in and there's no clunk in either the Big or Little Slot.

Then the quality of light changes and she stands at the door of her Separate Area.

"No goat tomorrow, I'm out of here and down the hill," she says. "I swear to God. You watch."

I go into my Separate Area and put on my footies. I have some cocoa and take out a Daily Partner Performance Evaluation Form.

Do I note any attitudinal difficulties? I do not. How do I rate my Partner overall? Very good. Are there any Situations which require Mediation?

There are not.

I fax it in.

3.

Next morning, no goat. Also no note. Janet sits on her log and smokes and together we wait to hear a clunk in the Big Slot.

No heads poke in and there's no clunk in either the Big or Little Slot.

About lunch we hit the Reserve Crackers. About dinner we again hit the Reserve Crackers.

Then the quality of light changes and she stands at the door of her Separate Area.

"Crackers, crackers, crackers!" she says pitifully. "Jesus, I wish you'd talk to me. I don't see why you won't. I'm about to go bonkers. We could at least talk. At least have some fun. Maybe play some Scrabble."

Scrabble.

I wave good night and give her a grunt.

"Bastard," she says, and hits me with the flint. She's a good thrower and I almost say ow. Instead I make a horse-like sound of fury and consider pinning her to the floor in an effort to make her submit to my superior power etc. etc. Then I go into my Separate Area. I put on my footies and tidy up. I have some cocoa. I take out a Daily Partner Performance Evaluation Form.

Do I note any attitudinal difficulties? I do not. How do I rate my Partner overall? Very good. Are there any Situations which require Mediation?

There are not.

I fax it in.

4.

In the morning in the Big Slot there's a nice fat goat. Also a note:

Ha ha! it says. *Sorry about the no goat and all. A little mix-up. In the future, when you look in here for a goat, what you will*

find on every occasion is a goat, and not a note. Or maybe both.
Ha ha! Happy eating! Everything's fine!

I skin the goat briskly with the flint. Janet comes in,
smiles when she sees the goat, and makes, very quickly, a
nice little fire, and does not say one English word all morning and even traces a few of our pictographs with a wet-
tened finger, as if awestruck at their splendid beauty and
so on.

Around noon she comes over and looks at the cut on
my arm, from where she threw the flint.

"You gonna live?" she says. "Sorry, man, really sorry, I
just like lost it."

I give her a look. She cans the English, then starts wailing in grief and sort of hunkers down in apology.

The goat tastes super after two days of crackers.

I have a nap by the fire and for once she doesn't walk
around singing pop hits in English, only mumbles unintel-
ligibly and pretends to be catching and eating small bugs.

Her way of saying sorry.

No one pokes their head in.

5.

Once, back in the days when people still poked their heads
in, this guy poked his head in.

"Whoa," he said. "These are some very cramped living
quarters. This really makes you appreciate the way we live
now. Do you have call-waiting? Do you know how to
make a nice mushroom cream sauce? Ha ha! I pity you

guys. And also, and yet, I thank you guys, who were my precursors, right? Is that the spirit? Is that your point? You weren't ignorant on purpose? You were doing the best you could? Just like I am? Probably someday some guy representing me will be in there, and some punk who I'm precursor of will be hooting at me, asking why my shoes were made out of dead cows and so forth? Because in that future time, wearing dead skin on your feet, no, they won't do that. That will seem to them like barbarity, just like you dragging that broad around by her hair seems to us like barbarity, although to me, not that much, after living with my wife fifteen years. Ha ha! Have a good one!"

I never drag Janet around by the hair.

Too cliché.

Just then his wife poked in her head.

"Stinks in there," she said, and yanked her head out.

"That's the roasting goat," her husband said. "Everything wasn't all prettied up. When you ate meat, it was like you were eating actual meat, the flesh of a dead animal, an animal that maybe had been licking your hand just a few hours before."

"I would never do that," said the wife.

"You do it now, bozo!" said the man. "You just pay someone to do the dirty work. The slaughtering? The skinning?"

"I do not either," said the wife.

We couldn't see them, only hear them through the place where the heads poke in.

"Ever heard of a slaughterhouse?" the husband said. "Ha ha! Gotcha! What do you think goes on in there?

Some guy you never met kills and flays a cow with what you might term big old cow eyes, so you can have your shoes and I can have my steak and my shoes!"

"That's different," she said. "Those animals were raised for slaughter. That's what they were made for. Plus I cook them in an oven, I don't squat there in my underwear with smelly smoke blowing all over me."

"Thank heaven for small favors," he said. "Joking! I'm joking. You squatting in your underwear is not such a bad mental picture, believe me."

"Plus where do they poop," she said.

"Ask them," said the husband. "Ask them where they poop, if you so choose. You paid your dime. That is certainly your prerogative."

"I don't believe I will," said the wife.

"Well, I'm not shy," he said.

Then there was no sound from the head-hole for quite some time. Possibly they were quietly discussing it.

"Okay, so where do you poop?" asked the husband, poking his head in.

"We have disposable bags that mount on a sort of rack," said Janet. "The septic doesn't come up this far."

"Ah," he said. "They poop in bags that mount on racks."

"Wonderful," said his wife. "I'm the richer for that information."

"But hold on," the husband said. "In the old times, like when the cave was real and all, where then did they go? I take it there were no disposal bags in those times, if I'm right."

"In those times they just went out in the woods," said Janet.

"Ah," he said. "That makes sense."

You see what I mean about Janet? When addressed directly we're supposed to cower shrieking in the corner but instead she answers twice in English?

I gave her a look.

"Oh, he's okay," she whispered. "He's no narc. I can tell."

In a minute in came a paper airplane: our Client Vignette Evaluation.

Under *Overall Impression* he'd written: *A-okay! Very nice.*

Under *Learning Value* he'd written: *We learned where they pooped. Both old days and now.*

I added it to our pile, then went into my Separate Area and put on my footies. I filled out my Daily Partner Performance Evaluation Form. Did I note any attitudinal difficulties? I did not. How did I rate my Partner overall? Very good. Were there any Situations which required Mediation?

There were not.

I faxed it in.

6.

This morning is the morning I empty our Human Refuse bags and the trash bags and the bag from the bottom of the sleek metal hole where Janet puts her used feminine items.

For this I get an extra sixty a month. Plus it's always nice to get out of the cave.

I knock on the door of her Separate Area.

"Who is it?" she asks, playing dumb.

She knows very well who it is. I stick in my arm and wave around a trash bag.

"Go for it," she says.

She's in there washing her armpits with a washcloth. The room smells like her, only more so. I add the trash from her wicker basket to my big white bag. I add her bag of used feminine items to my big white bag. I take three bags labeled Caution Human Refuse from the corner and add them to my big pink bag labeled Caution Human Refuse.

I mime to her that I dreamed of a herd that covered the plain like the grass of the earth, they were as numerous as grasshoppers and yet the meat of their humps resembled each a tiny mountain etc. etc., and sharpen my spear and try to look like I'm going into a sort of prehunt trance.

"Are you going?" she shouts. "Are you going now? Is that what you're saying?"

I nod.

"Christ, so go already," she says. "Have fun. Bring back some mints."

She has worked very hard these many months to hollow out a rock in which to hide her mints and her smokes. Mints mints mints. Smokes smokes smokes. No matter how long we're in here together I will never get the hots for her. She's fifty and has large feet and sloping shoulders and a pinched little face and chews with her mouth open. Sometimes she puts on big ugly glasses in the cave and does a crossword: very verboten.

Out I go, with the white regular trash bag in one hand and our mutual big pink Human Refuse bag in the other.

7.

Down in the blue-green valley is a herd of robotic something-or-others, bent over the blue-green grass, feeding I guess? Midway between our mountain and the opposing mountains is a wide green river with periodic interrupting boulders. I walk along a white cliff, then down a path marked by a yellow dot on a pine. Few know this way. It is a non-Guest path. No Attractions are down it, only Disposal Area 8 and a little Employees Only shop in a doublewide, a real blessing for us, we're so close and all.

Inside the doublewide are Marty and a lady we think is maybe Marty's wife but then again maybe not.

Marty's shrieking at the lady, who's writing down whatever he shrieks.

"Just do as they ask!" he shrieks, and she writes it down. "And not only that, do more than that, son, more than they ask! Excel! Why not excel? Be excellent! Is it bad to be good? Now son, I know you don't think that, because that is not what you were taught, you were taught that it is good to be good, I very clearly remember teaching you that. When we went fishing, and you caught a fish, I always said good, good fishing, son, and when you caught no fish, I frowned, I said bad, bad catching of fish, although I don't believe I was ever cruel about it. Are you getting this?"

"Every word," the lady says. "To me they're like nuggets of gold."

"Ha ha," says Marty, and gives her a long loving scratch on the back, and takes a drink of Squirt and starts shrieking again.

"So anyways, do what they ask!" he shrieks. "Don't you know how much we love you here at home, and want you to succeed? As for them, the big-wigs you wrote me about, freak them big-wigs! Just do what they ask though. In your own private mind, think what you like, only do what they ask, so they like you. And in this way, you will succeed. As for the little-wigs you mentioned, just how little are they? You didn't mention that. Are they a lot littler wig than you? In that case, freak them, ignore them if they talk to you, and if they don't talk to you, go up and start talking to them, sort of bossing them around, you know, so they don't start thinking they're the boss of you. But if they're the same wig as you, be careful, son! Don't piss them off, don't act like you're the boss of them, but also don't bend over for some little shit who's merely the same wig as you, or else he'll assume you're a smaller wig than you really actually are. As for friends, sure, friends are great, go ahead and make friends, they're a real blessing, only try to avoid making friends with boys who are the same or lesser wig than you. Only make friends with boys who are bigger wigs than you, assuming they'll have you, which probably they won't. Because why should they? Who are you? You're a smaller wig than them. Although then again, they might be slumming, which would be good for you, you could sneak right in there."

Marty gives me a little wave, then resumes shrieking.

"I don't want to put the pressure on, son," he says. "I know you got enough pressure, with school being so hard and all, and you even having to make your own book covers because of our money crunch, so I don't want to put on extra pressure by saying that the family honor is at stake, but guess what pal, it is! You're it, kid! You're as good as we got. Think of it, me and your mother, and Paw-Paw and Mee-Maw, and Great Paw-Paw, who came over here from wherever he was before, in some kind of boat, and fixed shoes all his life in a shack or whatever? Remember that? Why'd he do that? So you could eventually be born! Think of that! All those years of laundry and stuffing their faces and plodding to the market and making love and pushing out the babies and so on, and what's the upshot? You, pal, you're the freaking upshot. And now there you are, in boarding school, what a privilege, the first one of us to do it, so all's I'm saying is, do your best and don't take no shit from nobody, unless taking shit from them is part of your master plan to get the best of them by tricking them into being your friend. Just always remember who you are, son, you're a Kusacki, my only son, and I love you. Ack, I'm getting mushy here."

"You're doing great," says the lady.

"So much to say," he says.

"And Jeannine sends her love too," says the lady.

"And Jeannine sends her love too," he says. "For crissake's sake, Jeannine, write it down if you want to say it. I don't have to say it for you to write it. Just write it. You're my wife."

"I'm not your wife," says Jeannine.

"You are to me," says Marty, and she sort of leans into him and he takes another slug of the Squirt.

I buy Janet some smokes and mints and me a Kayo. I really like Kayo.

"Hey, you hear about Dave Wolley?" Marty says to me. "Dave Wolley from Wise Mountain Hermit? You know him? You know Dave?"

I know Dave very well. Dave was part of the group that used to meet for the barbecues at Russian Peasant Farm.

"Well, wave bye-bye to Dave," Marty says. "Wise Mountain Hermit is kaput. Dave is kaput."

"I've never seen Dave so upset," says Jeannine.

"He was very freaking upset," says Marty. "Who wouldn't be? He was superdedicated."

Dave was superdedicated. He grew his own beard long instead of wearing a fake and even when on vacation went around barefoot to make his feet look more like the feet of an actual mountain ascetic.

"The problem is, Wise Mountain Hermit was too far off the beaten path," Marty says. "Like all you Remotes. All you Remotes, you're too far off the beaten path. Think about it. These days we got very few Guests to begin with, which means we got even fewer Guests willing to walk way the hell up here to see you Remotes. Right? Am I right?"

"You are absolutely right," says Jeannine.

"I am absolutely right," says Marty. "Although I am not happy about being absolutely right, because if you think of it, if you Remotes go kaput, where am I? It's you Remotes

I'm servicing. See? Right? Give him his mints. Make change for the poor guy. He's got to get back to work."

"Have a good one," says Jeannine, and makes my change.

It's sad about Dave. Also it's worrisome. Because Wise Mountain Hermit was no more Remote than we are, plus it was much more popular, because Dave was so good at dispensing ad-libbed sage advice.

I walk down the path to the Refuse Center and weigh our Human Refuse. I put the paperwork and the fee in the box labeled Paperwork and Fees. I toss the trash in the dumpster labeled Trash, and the Human Refuse in the dumpster labeled Caution Human Refuse, then sit against a tree and drink my Kayo.

8.

Next morning in the Big Slot is a goat and in the Little Slot a rabbit and a note addressed to Distribution:

Please accept this extra food as a token of what our esteem is like, the note says. *Please know that each one of you is very special to us, and are never forgotten about. Please know that if each one of you could be kept, you would be, if that would benefit everyone. But it wouldn't, or we would do it, wouldn't we, we would keep every one of you. But as we meld into our sleeker new organization, what an excellent opportunity to adjust our Staff Mix. And so, although in this time of scarcity and challenge, some must perhaps go, the upside of this is, some must stay, and perhaps it will be you. Let us hope it* will *be you, each and every one of you, but no, as stated previously, it won't, that is impossible. So just enjoy the treats provided, and don't worry, and wait for your supervisor to contact you, and if he or she doesn't, know with relief that the Staff Remixing has passed by your door. Although it is only honest to inform you that some who make the first pass may indeed be removed in the second, or maybe even a third, depending on how the Remixing goes, although if anyone is removed in both the first and second pass, that will be a redundant screw-up, please ignore. We will only remove each of you once. If that many times! Some of you will be removed never, the better ones of you. But we find ourselves in a too-many-Indians situation and so must first cut some Indians and then, later, possibly, some chiefs. But not yet, because that is harder, because that is us. Soon, but not yet, we have to decide which of us to remove, and that is so very hard, because we are so very useful. Not that we are saying we chiefs are more useful than you Indians, but certainly we do make some very difficult decisions that perhaps you Indians would find hard to make, keeping you up nights, such as which of you to remove. But don't worry about us, we've been doing this for years, only first and foremost remember that what we are doing, all of us, chiefs and Indians both, is a fun privilege, how many would like to do what we do, in the entertainment field.*

Which I guess explains about Dave Wolley.

"Jeez," says Janet. "Let the freaking canning begin."

I give her a look.

"Oh all right all right," she says. "Ooga mooga. Ooga ooga mooga. Is that better?"

She can be as snotty as she likes but a Remixing is nothing to sneeze at.

I skin and roast the goat and rabbit. After breakfast she puts on her Walkman and starts a letter to her sister: very verboten. I work on the pictographs. I mean I kneel while pretending to paint them by dipping my crude dry brush into the splotches of hard colorful plastic meant to look like paint made from squashed berries.

Around noon the fax in my Separate Area makes the sound it makes when a fax is coming in.

Getting it would require leaving the cave and entering my Separate Area during working hours.

"Christ, go get it," Janet says. "Are you nuts? It might be from Louise."

I go get it.

It's from Louise.

Nelson doing better today, it says. *Not much new swelling. Played trucks and ate 3 pcs bologna. Asked about you. No temperature, good range of motion in both legs and arms. Visa is up to $6800, should I transfer to new card w/ lower interest rate?*

Sounds good, I fax back. *How are other kids?*

Kids are kids are kids, she faxes back. *Driving me nuts. Always talking.*

Miss you, I fax, and she faxes back the necessary Signature Card.

I sign the card. I fax the card.

Nelson's three. Three months ago his muscles stiffened up. The medicine they put him on to loosen his muscles did somewhat loosen them, but also it caused his muscles to swell. Otherwise he's fine, only he's stiff and swollen and it hurts when he moves. They have a name for what they originally thought he had, but when the medication made him swell up, Dr. Evans had to admit that whatever he had, it wasn't what they'd originally thought it was.

So we're watching him closely.

I return to the cave.

"How are things?" Janet says.

I grimace.

"Well, shit," she says. "You know I'm freaking rooting for you guys."

Sometimes she can be pretty nice.

9.

First thing next morning Greg Nordstrom pokes his head in and asks me to brunch.

Which is a first.

"How about me?" says Janet.

"Ha ha!" says Nordstrom. "Not you. Not today. Maybe soon, however!"

I follow him out.

Very bright sun.

About fifty feet from the cave there's a red paper screen that says Patience! Under Construction, and we go behind it.

"You'll be getting your proxy forms in your Slot soon," he says, spreading out some bagels on a blanket. "Fill out the proxy as you see fit, everything's fine, just vote, do it boldly, exert your choice, it has to do with your stock option. Are you vested? Great to be vested. Just wait until you are. It really feels like a Benefit. You'll see why they call Benefits Benefits, when every month, ka-ching, that option money kicks up a notch. Man, we're lucky."

"Yes," I say.

"I am and you are," he says. "Not everyone is. Some aren't. Those being removed in the Staff Remixing, no. But you're not being removed. At least I don't think so. Now Janet, I have some concerns about Janet, I don't know what they're going to do about Janet. It's not me, it's them, but what can I do? How is she? Is she okay? How have you found her? I want you to speak frankly. Are there problems? Problems we can maybe help correct? How is she? Nice? Reliable? It's not negative to point out a defect. Actually, it's positive, because then the defect can be fixed. What's negative is to withhold valuable info. Are you? Withholding valuable info? I hope not. Are you being negative? Is she a bit of a pain? Please tell me. I want you to. If you admit she's a bit of a pain, I'll write down how positive you were. Look, you know and I know she's got some performance issues, so what an exciting opportunity, for you to admit it and me to hear it loud and clear. Super!"

For six years she's been telling me about her Pap smears and her kid in rehab and her mother in Fort Wayne who has a bad valve and can't stand up or her lungs fill with blood etc. etc.

"I haven't really noticed any problems," I say.

"Blah blah blah," he says. "What kind of praise is that? Empty praise? Is it empty praise? I'd caution against empty praise. Because empty praise is what? Is like what? Is a lie. And a lie is what? Is negative. You're like the opposite of that little boy who cried Wolf. You're like that little boy who cried No Wolf, when a wolf was in fact chewing on his leg, by the name of Janet. Because what have I recently seen? Having seen your Daily Partner Performance Evaluation Forms, I haven't seen on them a single discouraging word. Not one. Did you ever note a single attitudinal difficulty? You did not. How did you rate your Partner overall? Very good, always, every single day. Were there ever any Situations which required Mediation? There were not, even when, in one instance, she told a guy where you folks pooped. In English. In the cave. I have documentation, because I read that guy's Client Vignette Evaluation."

It gets very quiet. The wind blows and the paper screen tips up a bit. The bagels look good but we're not eating them.

"Look," he says. "I know it's hard to be objective about people we come to daily know, but in the big picture, who benefits when the truth is not told? Does Janet? How can Janet know she's not being her best self if someone doesn't tell her, then right away afterwards harshly discipline her? And with Janet not being her best self, is the organization healthier? And with the organization not being healthier, and the organization being that thing that ultimately puts the food in your face, you can easily see that, by lying about Janet's behavior, you are taking the food out of your own face. Who puts the cash in your hand to buy that food in your face? We do. What do we want of you? We want you to tell the truth. That's it. That is all."

We sit awhile in silence.

"Very simple," he says. "A nonbrainer."

A white fuzzy thing lands in my arm hair. I pick it out.

Down it falls.

"Sad," he says. "Sad is all it is. We live in a beautiful world, full of beautiful challenges and flowers and birds and super people, but also a few regrettable bad apples, such as that questionable Janet. Do I hate her? Do I want her killed? Gosh no, I think she's super, I want her to be praised while getting a hot oil massage, she has some very nice traits. But guess what, I'm not paying her to have nice traits, I'm paying her to do consistently good work. Is she? Doing consistently good work? She is not. And here are you, saddled with a subpar colleague. Poor you. She's stopping your rise and growth. People are talking about you in our lounge. Look, I know you feel Janet's not so great. She's a lump to you. I see it in your eye. And that must chafe. Because you are good. Very good. One of our best. And she's bad, very bad, one of our worst, sometimes I could just slap her for what she's doing to you."

"She's a friend," I say.

"You know what it's like, to me?" he says. "The Bible. Remember that part in the Bible when Christ or God says that any group or organization of two or more of us is a body? I think that is so true. Our body has a rotten toe by the name of Janet, who is turning black and stinking up the joint, and next to that bad stinking toe lives her friend the good nonstinker toe, who for some reason insists on holding its tongue, if a toe can be said to have a tongue. Speak up, little toe, let the brain know the state of the rot, so we can rush down what is necessary to stop Janet from stinking. What will be needed? We do not yet know. Maybe some antiseptic, maybe a nice sharp saw with which to lop off Janet. For us to know, what must you do? Tell the truth. Start generating frank and nonbiased assessments of this subpar colleague. That's it. That is all. Did you or did you not in your Employment Agreement agree to complete, every day, an accurate Daily Partner Performance Evaluation Form? You did. You signed in triplicate. I have a copy in my dossier. But enough mean and sad talk, I know my point has been gotten. Gotten by you. Now for the fun. The eating. Eating the good food I have broughten. That's fun, isn't it? I think that's fun."

We start to eat. It's fun.

"Broughten," he says. "The good food I have broughten. Is it brought or broughten?"

"Brought," I say.

"The good food I have brought," he says. "Broughten."

10.

Back in the cave Janet's made a nice fire.

"So what did numbnuts want?" she says. "Are you fired?"

I shake my head no.

"Is he in love with you?" she says. "Does he want to go out with you?"

I shake my head no.

"Is he in love with me?" she says. "Does he want to go out with me? Am I fired?"

I do not shake my head no.

"Wait a minute, wait a minute, go back," she says. "I'm fired?"

I shake my head no.

"But I'm in the shit?" she says. "I'm somewhat in the shit?"

I shrug.

"Will you freaking talk to me?" she says. "This is important. Don't be a dick for once."

I do not consider myself a dick and I do not appreciate being called a dick, in the cave, in English, and the truth is, if she would try a little harder not to talk in the cave, she would not be so much in the shit.

I hold up one finger, like: Wait a sec. Then I go into my Separate Area and write her a note:

Nordstrom is unhappy with you, it says. *And unhappy with me because I have been lying for you on my DPPEFs. So I am going to start telling the truth. And as you know, if I tell the truth about you, you will be a goner, unless you start acting better. Therefore please start acting better. Sorry I couldn't say this in the cave, but as you know, we are not supposed to speak English in the cave. I enjoy working with you. We just have to get this thing straightened out.*

Sitting on her log she reads my note.

"Time to pull head out of ass, I guess," she says.

I give her a thumbs-up.

11.

Next morning I go to the Big Slot and find it goatless. Also there is no note.

Janet comes out and hands me a note and makes, very quickly, a nice little fire.

I really apreciate what you did, her note says. *That you tole me the truth. Your a real pal and are going to see how good I can be.*

For breakfast I count out twenty Reserve Crackers each. Afterward I work on the pictographs and she pretends to catch and eat small bugs. For lunch I count out twenty Reserve Crackers each. After lunch I pretend to sharpen my spear and she sits at my feet speaking long strings of unintelligible sounds.

No one pokes their head in.

When the quality of light changes she stands at the door of her Separate Area and sort of wiggles her eyebrows, like: Pretty good, eh?

I go into my Separate Area. I take out a Daily Partner Performance Evaluation Form.

For once it's easy.

Do I note any attitudinal difficulties? I do not. How do I rate my Partner overall? Very good. Are there any Situations which require Mediation?

There are not.

I fax it in.

12.

Next morning I go to the Big Slot and again find it goat-less. Again no note.

Janet comes out and again makes, very quickly, a nice little fire.

I count out twenty Reserve Crackers each. After breakfast we work on the pictographs. After lunch she goes to the doorway and starts barking out sounds meant to indicate that a very impressive herd of feeding things is thundering past etc. etc., which of course it is not, the feeding things, being robotic, are right where they always are, across the river. When she barks I grab my spear and come racing up and join her in barking at the imaginary feeding things.

All day no one pokes their head in.

Then the quality of light changes and she stands at the door of her Separate Area giving me a smile, like: It's actually sort of fun doing it right, isn't it?

I take out a Daily Partner Performance Evaluation Form.

Again: Easy.

Do I note any attitudinal difficulties? I do not. How do I rate my Partner overall? Very good. Are there any Situations which require Mediation?

There are not.

I fax it in.

Also I write Nordstrom a note:

Per our conversation, it says, *I took the liberty of bringing Janet up to speed. Since that time she has been doing wonderful work, as reflected in my (now truthful!!) Daily Partner Performance Evaluation Forms. Thank you for your frankness. Also, I apologize for that period during which I was less than truthful on my DPPEFs. I can see now just how negative that was.*

A bit of ass-kissing, yes.

But I've got some making up to do.

I fax it in.

13.

Late in the night my fax makes the sound it makes when a fax is coming in.

From Nordstrom:

What? What? it says. *You told her? Did I tell you to tell her? And now you have the nerve to say she is doing good? Why should I believe you when you say she is doing good, when all that time she was doing so bad you always said she was doing so good? Oh you have hacked me off. Do you know what I hate? Due to my childhood? Which is maybe why I'm so driven? A liar. Dad lied by cheating on Mom, Mom lied by cheating on Dad, with Kenneth, who was himself a liar, and promised, at his wedding to Mom, to buy me three ponies with golden saddles, and then later, upon divorcing Mom, promised to at least get me one pony with a regular saddle, but needless to say, no ponies were ever gotten by me. Which is maybe why I hate a liar. SO DON'T LIE ANY-*

MORE. Don't lie even one more time about that hideous Janet. I can't believe you told her! Do you really think I care about how she is? I KNOW how she is. She is BAD. But what I need is for you to SAY IT. For reasons of documentation. Do you have any idea how hard it is to fire a gal, not to mention an old gal, not to mention an old gal with so many years of service under her ancient withered belt? There is so much you don't know, about the Remixing, about our plans! Do not even answer me, I am too mad to read it.

Which is not at all what I had in mind.

No doubt my status with Nordstrom has been somewhat damaged.

But okay.

Janet is now doing better and I am now telling the truth. So things are as they should be.

And I'm sure that, in the long run, Nordstrom will come to appreciate what I've accomplished.

14.

Next morning I go to the Big Slot and again find it goatless. Again no note.

Janet comes out and makes, very quickly, a nice little fire.

We squat and eat our Reserve Crackers while occasionally swatting each other with our hands. We get in kind of a mock squabble and scurry around the cave bent over and shrieking. She is really doing very well. I pound a rock against a rock in rage, indicating that I intend to toss some dirt in her face. She barks back very sharply.

Someone pokes their head in.

Young guy, kind of goofy-looking.

"Bradley?" Janet says. "Holy shit."

"Hey, nice greeting, Ma," the guy says, and walks in. He's not supposed to walk in. No one's supposed to walk in. I can't remember a time when anyone has ever just walked in.

"Fucking stinks in here," he says.

"Don't you *even* come into my workplace and start swearing," Janet says.

"Yeah right Ma," he says. "Like you never came into my workplace and started swearing."

"Like you ever had a workplace," she says. "Like you ever worked."

"Like jewelry making wasn't work," he says.

"Oh Bradley you are so full of it," she says. "You didn't have none of the equipment and no freaking jewels. And no customers. You never made a single piece of jewelry. You just sat moping in the basement."

Just our luck: Our first Guest in two weeks and it's a relative.

I clear my throat. I give her a look.

"Give us five freaking minutes, will you, Mr. Tightass?" she says. "This is my kid here."

"I was conceptualizing my designs, Ma," he says. "Which is an important part of it. And you definitely swore at my workplace. I remember very clearly one time you came down into the basement and said I was a fucking asshole for wasting my time trying to make my dream come true of being a jewelry maker."

"Oh bullshit," she says. "I never once called you a ass-hole. And I definitely did not say fucking. I never say fuck. I quit that a long time ago. You ever hear me say fuck?"

She looks at me. I shake my head no. She never says fuck. When she means fuck she says freak. She is very very consistent about this.

"What?" says Bradley. "He don't talk?"

"He plays by the rules," she says. "Maybe you should try it sometime."

"I was trying," he says. "But still they kicked me out."

"Kicked you out of what?" she says. "Wait a minute, wait a minute, go back. They kicked you out of what? Of rehab?"

"It's nothing bad, Ma!" he shouts. "You don't have to make me feel ashamed about it. I feel bad enough, being called a thief by Mr. Doe in front of the whole group."

"Jesus, Bradley," she says. "How are you supposed to get better if you get kicked out of rehab? What did you steal this time? Did you steal a stereo again? Who's Mr. Doe?"

"I didn't steal nothing, Ma," he says. "Doe's my counselor. I borrowed something. A TV. The TV from the lounge. I just felt like I could get better a lot faster if I had a TV in my room. So I took control of my recovery. Is that so bad? I thought that's what I was there for, you know? I'm not saying I did everything perfect. Like I probably shouldn't of sold it."

"You sold it?" she says.

"There was nothing good ever on!" he says. "If they showed good programs I just know I would've gotten better. But no. It was so boring. So I decided to throw everybody a party, because they were all supporting me so well, by letting me keep the TV in my room? And so, you know, I sold the TV, for the party, and was taking the bucks over to the Party Place, to get some things for the party, some hats and tooters and stuff like that, but then I've got this problem, with substances, and so I sort of all of a sudden wanted some substances. And then I ran into this guy with some substances. That guy totally fucked me! By being there with those substances right when I had some money? He didn't care one bit about my recovery."

"You sold the rehab TV to buy drugs," she says.

"To buy substances, Ma, why can't you get it right?" he says. "The way we name things is important, Ma, Doe taught me that in counseling. Look, maybe you wouldn't have sold the TV, but you're not an inadvertent substance misuser, and guess what, I am, that's why I was in there. Do you hear me? I know you wish you had a perfect son, but you don't, you have an inadvertent substance misuser who sometimes makes bad judgments, like borrowing and selling a TV to buy substances."

"Or rings and jewels," says Janet. "My rings and jewels."

"Fuck Ma, that was a long time ago!" he says. "Why do you have to keep bringing that old shit up? Doe was so right. For you to win, I have to lose. Like when I was a kid and in front of the whole neighborhood you called me an animal torturer? That really hurt. That caused a lot of my problems. We were working on that in group right before I left."

"You were torturing a cat," she says. "With a freaking prod."

"A prod I built myself in metal shop," he says. "But of course you never mention that."

"A prod you were heating with a Sterno cup," she says.

"Go ahead, build your case," he says. "Beat up on me as much as you want, I don't have a choice. I have to be here."

"What do you mean, you have to be here?" she says.

"Ma, haven't you been listening?" he shouts. "I got kicked out of rehab!"

"Well you can't stay here," she says.

"I have to stay here!" he says. "Where am I supposed to go?"

"Go home," she says. "Go home with Grammy."

"With Grammy?" he says. "Are you kidding me? Oh God, the group would love this. You're telling a very troubled inadvertent substance misuser to go live with his terminally ill grandmother? You have any idea how stressful that would be for me? I'd be inadvertently misusing again in a heartbeat. Grammy's always like: Get me this, get me that, sit with me, I'm scared, talk with me, it hurts when I breathe. I'm twenty-four, Ma, baby-sitting brings me down. Plus she's kind of deranged? She sort of like hallucinates? I think it's all that blood in her lungs. The other night she woke up at midnight and said I was trying to steal something from her. Can you believe it? She's like all kooky! I wasn't stealing. Her necklaces got tangled up and

I was trying to untangle them. And Keough was trying to help me."

"Keough was at the house?" she says. "I thought I told you no Keough."

"Ma, Jesus Christ, Keough's my friend," he says. "Like my only friend. How am I supposed to get better without friends? At least I have one. You don't have any."

"I have plenty of friends," she says.

"Name one," he says.

She looks at me.

Which I guess is sort of sweet.

Although I don't see why she had to call me Mr. Tightass.

"Fine, Ma," he says. "You don't want me staying here, I won't stay here. You want me to inadvertently misuse substances, I'll inadvertently misuse substances. I'll turn tricks and go live in a ditch. Is that what you want?"

"Turn tricks?" she says. "Who said anything about turning tricks?"

"Keough's done it," he says. "It's what we eventually come to, our need for substances is so great. We can't help it."

"Well, I don't want you turning tricks," she says. "That I don't go for."

"But living in a ditch is okay," he says.

"If you want to live in a ditch, live in a ditch," she says.

"I don't want to live in a ditch," he says. "I want to turn my life around. But it would help me turn my life around if I had a little money. Like twenty bucks. So I can go back and get those party supplies. The tooters and all? I want to make it up to my friends."

"Is that was this is about?" she says. "You want money? Well I don't have twenty bucks. And you don't need tooters to have a party."

"But I want tooters," he says. "Tooters make it more fun."

"I don't have twenty bucks," she says.

"Ma, please," he says. "You've always been there for me. And I've got a bad feeling about this. Like this might be my last chance."

She pulls me off to one side.

"I'll pay you back on payday," she says.

I give her a look.

"Come on, man," she says. "He's my *son*. You know how it is. You got a sick kid, I got a sick kid."

My feeling is, yes and no. My sick kid is three. My sick kid isn't a con man.

Although at this point it's worth twenty bucks to get the guy out of the cave.

I go to my Separate Area and get the twenty bucks. I give it to her and she gives it to him.

"Excellent!" he says, and goes bounding out the door. "A guy can always count on his ma."

Janet goes straight to her Separate Area. The rest of the afternoon I hear sobbing.

Sobbing or laughing.

Probably sobbing.

When the quality of light changes I go to my Separate

Area. I make cocoa. I tidy up. I take out a Daily Partner Performance Evaluation Form.

This is really pushing it. Her kid comes into the cave in street clothes, speaks English in the cave, she speaks English back, they both swear many many times, she spends the whole afternoon weeping in her Separate Area.

Then again, what am I supposed to do, rat out a friend with a dying mom on the day she finds out her screwed-up son is even more screwed up than she originally thought?

Do I note any attitudinal difficulties? I do not. How do I rate my Partner overall? Very good. Are there any Situations which require Mediation?

There are not.

I fax it in.

15.

Late that night my fax makes the sound it makes when a fax is coming in.

From Louise:

Bad day, she says. *He had a fever then suddenly got very cold. And his legs are so swollen. In places the skin looks ready to split. Ate like two handfuls dry Chex all day. And whiny, oh my God the poor thing. Stood on the heat grate all day in his underwear, staring out the window. Kept saying where is Daddy, why is he never here? Plus the Evemplorine went up to $70 for 120 count. God, it's all drudge drudge drudge, you should see me, I look about ninety. Also a big strip of trim or siding came floating down as we* *were getting in the car and nearly killed the twins. Insurance said they won't pay. What do I do, do I forget about it? Will something bad happen to the wood underneath if we don't get it nailed back up? Ugh. Don't fax back, I'm going to sleep.*

Love, Me.

I get into bed and lie there counting and recounting the acoustic tiles on the ceiling of my darkened Separate Area.

One hundred forty-four.

Plus I am so hungry. I could kill for some goat.

Although certainly, dwelling on problems doesn't solve them. Although on the other hand, thinking positively about problems also doesn't solve them. But at least then you feel positive, which is, or should be, you know, empowering. And power is good. Power is necessary at this point. It is necessary at this point for me to be, you know, a rock. What I need to remember now is that I don't have to solve the problems of the world. It is not within my power to cure Nelson, it is only necessary for me to do what I can do, which is keep the money coming in, and in order for me to keep the money coming in, it is necessary for me to keep my chin up, so I can continue to do a good job. That is, it is necessary for me to avoid dwelling negatively on problems in the dark of night in my Separate Area, because if I do, I will be tired in the morning, and might then do a poor job, which could jeopardize my ability to keep the money coming in, especially if, for example, there is a Spot Check.

I continue to count the tiles but as I do it try to smile. I smile in the dark and sort of nod confidently. I try to positively and creatively imagine surprising and innovative solutions to my problems, like winning the Lotto, like the Remixing being discontinued, like Nelson suddenly one morning waking up completely cured.

16.

Next morning is once again the morning I empty our Human Refuse bags and the trash bags and the bag from the bottom of the sleek metal hole.

I knock on the door of her Separate Area.

"Enter," she says.

I step in and mime to her that I dreamed of a herd that covered the plain like the grass of the earth, they were as numerous as grasshoppers and yet the meat of their humps resembled each a tiny mountain etc. etc.

"Hey, sorry about yesterday," she says. "Really sorry. I never dreamed that little shit would have the nerve to come here. And you think he paid to get in? I very much doubt it. My guess is, he hopped the freaking fence."

I add the trash from her wicker basket to my big white bag. I add her bag of used feminine items to my big white bag.

"But he's a good-looking kid, isn't he?" she says.

I sort of curtly nod. I take three bags labeled Caution Human Refuse from the corner and add them to my big pink bag labeled Caution Human Refuse.

"Hey, look," she says. "Am I okay? Did you narc me out? About him being here?"

I give her a look, like: I should've but I didn't.

"Thank you *so* much," she says. "Damn, you're nice. From now on, no more screw-ups. I swear to God."

Out I go, with the white regular trash bag in one hand and our mutual big pink Human Refuse bag in the other.

17.

Nobody's on the path, although from the direction of Pioneer Encampment I hear the sound of rushing water, possibly the Big Durn Flood? Twice a month they open up the Reserve Tanks and the river widens and pretty soon some detachable house parts and Pioneer wagons equipped with special inflatable bladders float by, while from their P.A. we dimly hear the sound of prerecorded screaming Settlers.

I walk along the white cliff, turn down the non-Guest path marked by the little yellow dot, etc. etc.

Marty's out front of the doublewide playing catch with a little kid.

I sit against a tree and start my paperwork.

"Great catch, son!" Marty says to the kid. "You can really catch. I would imagine you're one of the very best catchers in that school."

"Not exactly, Dad," the kid says. "Those kids can really catch. Most of them catch even better than me."

"You know, in a way I'm glad you might quit that school," says Marty. "Those rich kids. I'm very unsure about them."

"I don't want to quit," says the kid. "I like it there."

"Well, you might have to quit," says Marty. "We might make the decision that it's best for you to quit."

"Because we're running out of money," says the kid.

"Yes and no," says Marty. "We are and we aren't. Daddy's job is just a little, ah, problematical. Good catch! That is an excellent catch. Pick it up. Put your glove back on. That was too hard a throw. I knocked your glove off."

"I guess I have a pretty weak hand," the kid says.

"Your hand is perfect," says Marty. "My throw was too hard."

"It's kind of weird, Dad," the kid says. "Those kids at school are better than me at a lot of things. I mean, like everything? Those kids can really catch. Plus some of them went to camp for baseball and camp for math. Plus you should see their clothes. One kid won a trophy in golf. Plus they're nice. When I missed a catch they were really really nice. They always said, like, Nice try. And they tried to teach me? When I missed at long division they were nice. When I ate with my fingers they were nice. When my shoes split in gym they were nice. This one kid gave me his shoes."

"He gave you his shoes?" says Marty.

"He was really nice," explains the kid.

"What were your shoes doing splitting?" says Marty. "Where did they split? Why did they split? Those were perfectly good shoes."

"In gym," says the kid. "They split in gym and my foot fell out. Then that kid who switched shoes with me wore them with his foot sticking out. He said he didn't mind.

And even with his foot sticking out he beat me at running. He was really nice."

"I heard you the first time," says Marty. "He was really nice. Maybe he went to being-nice camp. Maybe he went to giving-away-shoes camp."

"Well, I don't know if they have that kind of camp," says the kid.

"Look, you don't need to go to a camp to know how to be nice," says Marty. "And you don't have to be rich to be nice. You just have to be nice. Do you think you have to be rich to be nice?"

"I guess so," says the kid.

"No, no, no," says Marty. "You don't. That's my point. You don't have to be rich to be nice."

"But it helps?" says the kid.

"No," says Marty. "It makes no difference. It has nothing to do with it."

"I think it helps," says the kid. "Because then you don't have to worry about your shoes splitting."

"Ah bullshit," says Marty. "You're not rich but you're nice. See? You were nice, weren't you? When someone else's shoes split, you were nice, right?"

"No one else's shoes ever split," says the kid.

"Are you trying to tell me you were the only kid in that whole school whose shoes ever split?" says Marty.

"Yes," says the kid.

"I find that hard to believe," says Marty.

"Once this kid Simon?" says the kid. "His pants ripped."

"Well, there you go," says Marty. "That's worse. Because

your underwear shows. Your pants never ripped. Because I
bought you good pants. Not that I'm saying the shoes
I bought you weren't good. They were very good. Among
the best. So what did this Simon kid do? When his pants
ripped? Was he upset? Did the other kids make fun of him?
Did he start crying? Did you rush to his defense? Did you
sort of like console him? Do you know what console
means? It means like say something nice. Did you say
something nice when his pants ripped?"

"Not exactly," the kid says.

"What did you say?" says Marty.

"Well, that boy, Simon, was a kind of smelly boy?" says
the kid. "He had this kind of smell to him?"

"Did the other kids make fun of his smell?" says Marty.

"Sometimes," says the kid.

"But they didn't make fun of your smell," says Marty.

"No," says the kid. "They made fun of my shoes
splitting."

"Too bad about that smelly kid though," says Marty.
"You gotta feel bad about a kid like that. What were his
parents thinking? Didn't they teach him how to wash? But
you at least didn't make fun of his smell. Even though the
other kids did."

"Well, I sort of did," the kid says.

"When?" says Marty. "On the day his pants ripped?"

"No," the kid says. "On the day my shoe split."

"Probably he was making fun of you on that day," sug-
gests Marty.

"No," the kid says. "He was just kind of standing there.
But a few kids were looking at my shoe funny. Because my

foot was poking out? So I asked Simon why he smelled so bad."

"And the other kids laughed?" says Marty. "They thought that was pretty good? What did he say? Did he stop making fun of your shoes?"

"Well, he hadn't really started yet," the kid says. "But he was about to."

"I bet he was," says Marty. "But you stopped him dead in his tracks. What did he say? After you made that crack about his smell?"

"He said maybe he did smell but at least his shoes weren't cheap," says the kid.

"So he turned it around on you," says Marty. "Very clever. The little shit. But listen, those shoes weren't cheap. I paid good money for those shoes."

"Okay," says the kid, and throws the ball into the woods.

"Nice throw," says Marty. "Very powerful."

"Kind of crooked though," says the kid, and runs off into the woods to get the ball.

"My kid," Marty says to me. "Home on break from school. We got him in boarding school. Only the best for my kid! Until they close us down, that is. You heard anything? Anything bad? I heard they might be axing Sheep May Safely Graze. So that's like fifteen shepherds. Which would kill me. I get a lot of biz off those shepherds. Needless to say, I am shitting bricks. Because if they close me, what do you think happens to that kid out there in the woods right now? Boarding school? You think boarding school happens? In a pig's ass. Boarding school does not happen, the opposite of boarding school happens, and he will be very freaking upset."

The kid comes jogging out of the woods with the ball in his hand.

"What are you talking about?" he says.

"About you," Marty says, and puts the kid in a head-lock. "About how great you are. How lovable you are."

"Oh that," the kid says, and smiles big.

18.

That night around nine I hear a sort of shriek from Janet's Separate Area.

A shriek, and then what sounds like maybe sobbing.

Then some louder sobbing and maybe something breaking, possibly her fax?

I go to her door and ask is she okay and she tells me go away.

I can't get back to sleep. So I fax Louise.

Everything okay? I write.

In about ten minutes a fax comes back.

Did Dr. Evans ever say anything about complete loss of mobil-ity? it says. *I mean complete. Today I took the kids to the park and let Ace off the leash and he saw a cat and ran off. When I came back from getting Ace, Nelson was like stuck inside this crawling tube. Like he couldn't stand up? Had no power in his legs. I mean none. That fucking Ace. If you could've seen Nelson's face. God. When I picked him up he said he thought I'd gone home without him. The poor thing. Plus he had to pee. And so he'd sort of peed himself. Not much, just a little. Other than that all is well, please don't worry. Well worry a little. We are at the end of our rope or however you say it, I'm already deep into the overdraft account and it's only the 5th. Plus I'm so tired at night I can't get to the bills and last time I paid late fees on both Visas and the MasterCard, thirty bucks a pop, those bastards, am thinking about just sawing off my arm and mailing it in. Ha ha, not really, I need that arm to sign checks.*

Love, Me.

From Janet's Separate Area come additional sobbing and some angry shouting.

I fax back:

Did you take him to Dr. Evans? I say.

Duh, she faxes back. *Have appt for Weds, will let you know. Don't worry, just do your job and also Nelson says hi and you're the best dad ever.*

Tell him hi and he's the best kid, I fax back.

What about the other kids? she faxes back.

Tell them they're also the best kids, I fax back.

From Janet's Separate Area comes the sound of Janet pounding on something repeatedly, probably her desk, presumably with her fist.

19.

Next morning in the Big Slot is no goat. Just a note.

From Janet:

Not coming in, it says. *Bradley lied about the tooters and bought some you-know-what. Big suprise right? Is in jail. Stupid dumbass. Got a fax last night. Plus my Ma's worse. Before she couldnt get up or her lungs filled with blood? Well now they fill with blood unless she switchs from side to side and who's there to switch her? Before Mrs Finn was but now Mrs Finn got a day-job so no more. So now I have to find someone and pay someone. Ha ha very funny, like I can aford that. Plus Bradley's bail which be-leve me I have defnitely considered not paying. With all this going on no way am I caving it up today. I'm sorry but I just cant, don't narc me out, okay? Just this one last time. I'm taking a Sick Day.*

She can't do that. She can't take a Sick Day if she's not sick. She can't take a Sick Day because she's sad about someone she loves being sick. And she certainly can't take a Sick Day because she's sad about someone she loves being in jail.

I count out ten Reserve Crackers and work all morning on the pictographs.

Around noon the door to her Separate Area flies open. She looks weird. Her hair is sticking up and she's wearing an I'm With Stupid sweatshirt over her cavewoman robe and her breath smells like whiskey.

Janet is wasted? Wasted in the cave?

"What I have here in this album?" she says. "Baby pictures of that fucking rat Bradley. Back when I loved him so much. Back before he was a druggie. See how cute? See how smart he looked?"

She shows me the album. He actually does not look cute or smart. He looks the same as he looked the other day, only smaller. In one picture he's sitting on a tricycle looking like he's planning a heist. In another he's got a sour look on his face and his hand down some smaller kid's diaper.

"God, you just love the little shits no matter what, don't you?" she says. "You know what I'm saying? If Bradley's dad woulda stuck around it might've been better. Bradley never knew him. I always used to say he took one look at Bradley and ran off. Maybe I shouldn't of said that. At least not in front of Bradley. Wow. I've had a few snorts. You want a snort? Come on, live a little! Take a Sick Day like me. I had three BallBusters and half a bottle of wine. This is the best Sick Day I ever took."

I guide her back to her Separate Area and push her sternly in.

"Come on in!" she says. "Have a BallBuster. You want one? I'm lonely in here. You want a BallBuster, Señor Tightass?"

I do not want a BallBuster.

What I want is for her to stay in her Separate Area keeping very quiet until she sobers up.

All day I sit alone in the cave. When the quality of light changes I go into my Separate Area and take out a Daily Partner Performance Evaluation Form.

When I was a kid, Dad worked at Kenner Beef. Loins would drop from this belt and he'd cut through this purple tendon and use a sort of vise to squeeze some blood into a graduated beaker for testing, then wrap the loin in a sling and swing it down to Finishing. Dad's partner was Fred Lank. Lank had a metal plate in his skull and went into these funks where he'd forget to cut the purple tendon and fail to squeeze out the blood and instead of placing the loin in the sling would just sort of drop the loin down on Finishing. When Lank went into a funk, Dad would cover for him by doing double loins. Sometimes Dad would do double loins for days at a time. When Dad died, Lank sent Mom a check for a thousand dollars, with a note:

Please keep, it said. *The man did so much for me.*

Which is I think part of the reason I'm having trouble ratting Janet out.

Do I note any attitudinal difficulties? I do not. How do I rate my Partner overall? Very good. Are there any Situations which require Mediation?

There are not.

I fax it in.

20.

Next morning in the Big Slot is no goat, just a note:

A question has arisen, it says. *Hence this note about a touchy issue that is somewhat grotesque and personal, but we must address it, because one of you raised it, the issue of which was why do we require that you Remote Attractions pay the money which we call, and ask that you call, the Disposal Debit, but which you people insist on wrongly calling the Shit Fee. Well, this is to tell you why, although isn't it obvious to most? We hope. But maybe not. Because what we have found, no offense, is that sometimes you people don't get things that seem pretty obvious to us, such as why you have to pay for your Cokes in your fridge if you drink them. Who should then? Did we drink your Cokes you drank? We doubt it. You did it. Likewise with what you so wrongly call* the Shit Fee, because why do you expect us to pay to throw away your poop when after all you made it? Do you think your poop is a legitimate business expense? Does it provide benefit to us when you defecate? No, on the contrary, it would provide benefit if you didn't, because then you would be working more. Ha ha! That is a joke. We know very well that all must poop. We grant you that. But also, as we all know, it takes time to poop, some more than others. As we get older, we notice this, don't you? Not that we're advocating some sort of biological plug or chemical constipator. Not yet, anyway! No, that would be wrong, we know that, and unhealthy, and no doubt some of you would complain about having to pay for the constipators, expecting us to provide them gratis.

That is another funny thing with some of you, we notice it, namely that, not ever having been up here, in our shoes, you always want something for nothing. You just don't get it! When you poop and it takes a long time and you are on the clock, do you ever see us outside looking mad with a stopwatch? So therefore please stop saying to us: I have defecated while on the clock, dispose of it for free, kindly absorb my expense. We find that loopy. Because, as you know, you Remote Locations are far away, and have no pipes, and hence we must pay for the trucks. The trucks that drive your poop. Your poop to the pipes. Why are you so silly? It is as if you expect us to provide those Cokes for free, just because you thirst. Do Cokes grow on trees? Well, the other thing that does not grow on a tree is a poop truck. Perhaps someone should explain to you the idea of how we do things, which is to make money. And why? Is it greed? Don't make us laugh. It is not. If we make money, we can grow, if we can grow, we can expand, if we can expand, we *can continue to employ you, but if we shrink, if we shrink or stay the same, woe to you, we would not be vital. And so help us help you, by not whining about your Disposal Debit, and if you don't like how much it costs, try eating less.*

And by the way, we are going to be helping you in this, by henceforth sending less food. We're not joking, this is austerity. We think you will see a substantial savings in terms of your Disposal Debits, as you eat less and your Human Refuse bags get smaller and smaller. And that, our friends, is a substantial savings that we, we up here, will not see, and do you know why not? I mean, even if we were eating less, which we already have decided we will not be? In order to keep our strength up? So we can continue making sound decisions? But do you know why we will not see the substantial savings you lucky ducks will? Because, as some of you have already grumbled about, we pay no Shit Fee, those of us up here. So that even if we shat less, we would realize no actual savings. And why do we pay no Shit Fee? Because that was negotiated into our contracts at Time-of-Hire. What would you have had us do? Negotiate inferior contracts? Act against our own healthy self-interest? Don't talk crazy. Please talk sense. Many of us have Student Loans to repay. Times are hard, entire Units are being eliminated, the Staff Remixing continues, so no more talk of defecation flaring up, please, only let's remember that we are a family, and you are the children, not that we're saying you're immature, only that you do most of the chores while we do all the thinking, and also that we, in our own way, love you.

For several hours Janet does not come out.

Probably she is too hungover.

Around eleven she comes out, holding her copy of the memo.

"So what are they saying?" she says. "Less food? Even less food than now?"

I nod.

"Jesus Christ," she says. "I'm starving as it is."

I give her a look.

"I know, I know, I fucked up," she says. "I was a little buzzed. A little buzzed in the cave. Boo-hoo. Don't tell me, you narced me out, right? Did you? Of course you did."

I give her a look.

"You didn't?" she says. "Wow. You're even nicer than I thought. You're the best, man. And starting right now, no more screw-ups. I know I said that before. But this time, for real. You watch."

Just then there's a huge clunk in the Big Slot.

"Excellent!" she says. "I hope it's a big thing of Motrin."

But it's not a big thing of Motrin. It's a goat. A weird-looking goat. Actually a plastic goat. With a predrilled hole for the spit to go through. In the mouth is a Baggie and in the Baggie is a note:

In terms of austerity, it says. *No goat today. In terms of verisimilitude, mount this fake goat and tend as if real. Mount well above fire to avoid burning. In event of melting, squelch fire. In event of burning, leave area, burning plastic may release harmful fumes.*

I mount the fake goat on the spit and Janet sits on the boulder with her head in her hands.

21.

Next morning is once again the morning I empty our Human Refuse bags and the trash bags and the bag from the bottom of the sleek metal hole where Janet puts her used feminine items.

I knock on the door of her Separate Area.

Janet slides the bags out, all sealed and labeled and ready to go.

"Check it out," she says. "I'm a new woman."

Out I go, with the white regular trash bag in one hand and our mutual big pink Human Refuse bag in the other.

I walk along the white cliff, then down the path marked by the small yellow dot on the pine etc. etc.

On the door of Marty's doublewide is a note:

Due to circumstances beyond our control we are no longer here, it says. *But please know how much we appreciated your patronage. As to why we are not here, we will not comment on that, because we are bigger than that. Bigger than some people. Some people are snakes. To some people, fifteen years of good loyal service means squat. All's we can say is, watch your damn backs.*

All the best and thanks for the memories,

Marty and Jeannine and little Eddie.

Then the door flies open.

Marty and Jeannine and little Eddie are standing there holding suitcases.

"Hello and good-bye," says Marty. "Feel free to empty your shit bag inside the store."

"Now, Marty," says Jeannine. "Let's try and be positive about this, okay? We're going to do fine. You're too good for this dump anyway. I've always said you were too good for this dump."

"Actually, Jeannine," Marty says. "When I first got this job you said I was lucky to even get a job, because of my dyslexia."

"Well, honey, you are dyslexic," says Jeannine.

"I never denied being dyslexic," says Marty.

"He writes his letters and numbers backwards," Jeannine says to me.

"What are you, turning on me, Jeannine?" Marty says. "I lose my job and you turn on me?"

"Oh Marty, I'm not turning on you," Jeannine says. "I'm not going to stop loving you just because you've got troubles. Just like you've never stopped loving me, even though I've got troubles."

"She gets too much spit in her mouth," Marty says to me.

"Marty!" says Jeannine.

"What?" Marty says. "You can say I'm dyslexic, but I can't say you get too much spit in your mouth?"

"Marty, please," she says. "You're acting crazy."

"I'm not acting crazy," he says. "It's just that you're turning on me."

"Don't worry about me, Dad," the kid says. "I won't turn on you. And I don't mind going back to my old school. Really I don't."

"He had a little trouble with mean kids in his old school," Marty says to me. "Which is why we switched him. Although nothing you couldn't handle, right, kid? Actually, I think it was good for him. Taught him toughness."

"As long as nobody padlocks me to the boiler again," the kid says. "That part I really didn't like. Wow, those rats or whatever."

"I doubt those were actual rats," says Marty. "More than likely they were cats. The janitor's cats. My guess is, it was dark in that boiler room and you couldn't tell a cat from a rat."

"The janitor didn't have any cats," the kid says. "And he said I was lucky those rats didn't start biting my pants. Because of the pudding smell. From when those kids pinned me down and poured pudding down my pants."

"Was that the same day?" Marty says. "The rats and the pudding? I guess I didn't realize them two things were on the same day. Wow, I guess you learned a lot of toughness on that day."

"I guess so," the kid says.

"But nothing you couldn't handle," Marty says.

"Nothing I couldn't handle," the kid says, and blinks, and his eyes water up.

"Well, Christ," Marty says, and his eyes also water up. "Time to hit the road, family. I guess this it. Let's say our good-byes. Our good-byes to Home Sweet Home."

They take a little tour around the doublewide and do a family hug, then drag their suitcases down the path.

I go to the Refuse Center and weigh our Human Refuse. I put the paperwork and the fee in the box labeled Paperwork and Fees. I toss the trash in the dumpster labeled Trash, and the Human Refuse in the dumpster labeled Caution Human Refuse.

I feel bad for Marty and Jeannine, and especially I feel bad for the kid.

I try to imagine Nelson padlocked to a boiler in a dark room full of rats.

Plus now where are us Remotes supposed to go for our smokes and mints and Kayos?

22.

Back at the cave Janet is working very industriously on the pictographs.

As I come in she points to my Separate Area while mouthing the word: Fax.

I look at her. She looks at me.

She mouths the words: Christ, go. Then she holds one hand at knee level, to indicate Nelson.

I go.

But it's not for me, it's for her.

Ms. Foley's fax appears to be inoperative? the cover letter says. *Kindly please forward the attached.*

Please be informed, the attached fax says, *I did my very best in terms of your son, and this appeared, in my judgment, to be an excellent plea bargain, which, although to some might appear disadvantageous, ten years is not all that long when you consider all the bad things that he has done. But he was happy enough about it, after some initial emotions such as limited weeping, and thanked me for my hard work, although not in those exact words, as he was fairly, you know, upset. On a personal note, may I say how sorry I am, but also that in the grand scheme of things such as geology ten years is not so very long really.*

Sincerely,

Evan Joeller, Esq.

I take the fax out to Janet, who reads it while sitting on her log.

She's sort of a slow reader.

When she's finally done she looks crazy and for a minute I think she's going to tear the cave apart but instead she scoots into the corner and starts frantically pretending to catch and eat small bugs.

I go over and put my hand on her shoulder, like: Are you okay?

She pushes my hand away roughly and continues to pretend to catch and eat small bugs.

Just then someone pokes their head in.

Young guy, round head, expensive-looking glasses.

"Bibby, hand me up Cole," he says. "So he can see. Cole-Cole, can you see? Here. Daddy will hold you up."

A little kid's head appears alongside the dad's head.

"Isn't this cool, Cole?" says the dad. "Aren't you glad Mommy and Daddy brought you? Remember Daddy told you? How people used to live in caves?"

"They did not," the little boy says. "You're wrong."

"Bibby, did you hear that?" the dad says. "He just said I'm wrong. About people living in caves."

"I heard it," says a woman from outside. "Cole, people really did use to live in caves. Daddy's not wrong."

"Daddy's always wrong," says the little boy.

"He just said I'm always wrong," the dad says. "Did you hear that? Did you write that down? In the memory book? Talk about assertive! I should be so assertive. Wouldn't Norm and Larry croak if I was suddenly so assertive?"

"Well, it couldn't hurt you," the mom says.

"Believe me, I know," the dad says. "That's why I said it. I know very well I could afford to be more assertive. I was making a joke. Like an ironic joke at my own expense."

"I want to stab you, Dad," says the little boy. "With a sharp sword, you're so dumb."

"Ha ha!" says the dad. "But don't forget, Cole-Cole, the pen is mightier than the sword! Remember that? Remember I taught you that? Wouldn't it be better to compose an insulting poem, if you have something negative about me you want to convey? Now that's real power! Bibby, did you hear what he said? And then what I said? Did you write all that down? Also did you save that Popsicle wrapper? Did you stick it in the pocket in the back cover of the memory book and write down how cute he looked eating it?"

"What your name?" the little boy yells at me.

I cower and shriek in the corner etc. etc.

"What your name I said!" the little boy shouts at me. "I hate you!"

"Now, Cole-Cole," says the dad. "Let's not use the word hate, okay, buddy? Remember what I told you? About hate being the nasty dark crayon and love being the pink? And remember what I told you about the clanging gong? And remember I told you about the bad people in the old days, who used to burn witches, and how scary that must've been for the witches, who were really just frightened old ladies who'd made the mistake of being too intelligent for the era they were living in?"

"You are not acceptable!" the kid shouts at me.

"Ha ha, oh my God!" says the dad. "Bibby, did you get that? Did you write that down? He's imitating us. Because we say that to him? Write down how mad he is. Look how red his face is! Look at him kick his feet. Wow, he is really pissed. Cole, good persistence! Remember how Daddy told you about the little train that could? How everyone kept trying to like screw it and not give it its due, and how finally it got really mad and stomped its foot and got its way? Remember I told you about Chief Joseph, who never stopped walking? You're like him. My brave little warrior. Bibby, give him a juice box. Also he's got some goo-goo coming out of his nosehole."

"Jesus Christ," Janet mumbles.

I give her my sternest look.

"What was that?" says the dad. "I'm sorry, I didn't hear you. What did you just say?"

"Nothing," Janet says. "I didn't say nothing."

"I heard you very clearly," says the dad. "You said Jesus Christ. You said Jesus Christ because of what I said about the goo-goo in my son's nosehole. Well, first of all, I'm sorry if you find a little boy's nosehole goo-goo sickening, it's perfectly normal, if you had a kid of your own you'd know that, and second of all, since when do cavepeople speak English and know who Jesus Christ is? Didn't the cavepeople predate Christ, if I'm not mistaken?"

"Of course they did," the mom says from outside. "We just came from Christ. Days of Christ. And we're going backwards. Towards the exit."

"Look, pal, I got a kid," says Janet. "I seen plenty of snot. I just never called it goo-goo. That's all I'm saying."

"Bibby, get this," the dad says. "Parenting advice from the cavelady. The cavelady apparently has some strong opinions on booger nomenclature. For this I paid eighty bucks? If I want somebody badly dressed to give me a bunch of lip I can go to your mother's house."

"Very funny," says the mom.

"I meant it funny," says the dad.

"I was a good mom," Janet says. "My kid is as good as anybody's kid."

"Hey, share it with us," says the dad.

"Even if he is in jail," says Janet.

"Bibby, get this," says the dad. "The cavelady's kid is in jail."

"Don't you *even* make fun of my kid, you little suck-ass," says Janet.

"The cavelady just called you a suckass," says the mom.

"A little suckass," says the dad. "And don't think I'm going to forget it."

Soon flying in through the hole where the heads poke in is our wadded-up Client Vignette Evaluation.

Under *Learning Value* he's written: *Disastrous. We learned that some caveladies had potty mouths. I certainly felt like I was in the actual Neanderthal days. Not!*

Under *Overall Impression* he's written: *The cavelady called*

*me a suckass in front of my child. Thanks so much! A tremendous
and offensive waste of time. LOSE THE CAVELADY, SHE
IS THE WORST.*

"Know what I'm doing now?" the guy says. "I'm walking my copy down to the main office. Your ass is grass,
lady."

"Oh shit," Janet says, and sits on the log. "Shit shit shit.
I really totally blew it, didn't I?"

My God, did she ever. She really totally blew it.

"What are you going to do, man?" Janet says. "Are you
going to narc me out?"

I give her a look, like: Will you just please shut up?

The rest of the day we sit on our respective logs.

When the quality of light changes I go to my Separate
Area and take out a Daily Partner Performance Evaluation
Form.

A note comes sliding under my door.

I have a idea, it says. *Maybe you could say that ashole made
it all up? Like he came in and tried to get fresh with me and when
I wouldnt let him he made it up? That could work. I think it could
work. Please please don't narc me out, if I get fired I'm dead, you
know all the shit that's going on with me, plus you have to admit
I was doing pretty good before this.*

She was doing pretty good before this.

I think of Nelson. His wispy hair and crooked nose.
When I thank him for bravely taking all his medications
he always rests his head on my shoulder and says, No problem. Only he can't say his *r*'s. So it's like: No pwoblem. And
then he pats my belly, as if I'm the one who bravely took
all my medications.

Do I note any attitudinal difficulties?

I write: *Yes.*

How do I rate my Partner overall?

I write: *Poor.*

Are there any Situations which require Mediation?

I write: *Today Janet unfortunately interacted negatively with a Guest. Today Janet swore at a Guest in the cave. Today Janet unfortunately called a Guest a "suckass," in English, in the cave.*

I look it over.

It's all true.

I fax it in.

23.

A few minutes later my fax makes the sound it makes when a fax is coming in.

From Nordstrom:

This should be sufficient! it says. *Super! More than sufficient. Good for you. Feel no guilt. Are you Janet? Is Janet you? I think not. I think that you are you and she is she. You guys are not the same entity. You are distinct. Is her kid your kid? Is your kid her kid? No, her kid is her kid and your kid is your kid. Have you guilt? About what you have done? Please do not. Please have pride. What I suggest? Think of you and Janet as branches on a tree. While it's true that a branch sometimes needs to be hacked off and come floating down, so what, that is only one branch, it does not kill the tree, and sometimes one branch must die so that the others may live. And anyway, it only looks like death, because you are falsely looking at this through the lens of an individual*

limb or branch, when in fact you should be thinking in terms of
the lens of what is the maximum good for the overall organism,
our tree. When we chop one branch, we all become stronger! And
that branch on the ground, looking up, has the pleasure of know-
ing that he or she made the tree better, which I hope Janet will
do. Although knowing her? With her crappy attitude? Probably
she will lie on the ground wailing and gnashing her leaves while
saying swear words up at us. But who cares! She is gone. She is
a goner. And we have you to thank. So thanks! This is the way
organizations grow and thrive, via small courageous contributions
by cooperative selfless helpers, who are able to do that hardest of
things, put aside the purely personal aspect in order to see the big
picture. Oh and also, you might want to be out of the cave around
ten, as that is when the deed will be done.

Thanks so much!

Greg N.

I lie there counting and recounting the acoustic tiles
on the ceiling of my darkened Separate Area.

One hundred forty-four.

24.

Next morning is not the morning I empty our Human
Refuse bags and the trash bags and the bag from the bottom of the sleek metal hole, but I get up extremely early,
in fact it is still dark, and leave Janet a note saying I've gone
to empty our Human Refuse bags and our trash bags and
the bag from the bottom of her sleek metal hole etc. etc.,
then very quietly sneak out of the cave and cross the river

via wading and sit among the feeding things, facing away from the cave.

I sit there a long time.

When I get back, Janet's gone and the door to her Separate Area is hanging open and her Separate Area is completely empty.

Except for a note taped to the wall:

You freak you break my heart, it says. *Thanks a million. What the fuck am I supposed to do now? I guess I will go home and flip Ma from side to side until she dies from starving to death because we got no money. And then maybe I will hore myself with a jail gard to get Bradley out. I cant beleve after all this time you tern on me. And here I thought you were my frend but you were only interested in your own self. Not that I blame you. I mean, I do and I dont. Actually I do.*

You bastard,

Janet.

There are several big clunks in the Big Slot.

A goat, some steaks, four boxes of hash browns, caramel corn in a metal tub, several pies, bottles of Coke and Sprite, many many small containers of Kayo.

I look at that food a long time.

Then I stash it in my Separate Area, for later use.

For lunch I have a steak and hash browns and some pie and a Kayo.

Eating hash browns and pie and drinking Kayo in the cave is probably verboten but I feel I've somewhat earned it.

I clean up the mess. I sit on the log.

Around two there is a little tiny click in the Little Slot.

25.

A memo, to Distribution:

Regarding the rumors you may have lately been hearing, it says. *Please be advised that they are false. They are so false that we considered not even bothering to deny them. Because denying them would imply that we have actually heard them. Which we haven't. We don't waste our time on such nonsense. And yet we know that if we don't deny the rumors we haven't heard, you will assume they are true. And they are so false! So let us just categorically state that all the rumors you've been hearing are false. Not only the rumors you've heard, but also those you haven't heard, and even those that haven't yet been spread, are false. However, there is one exception to this, and that is if the rumor is good. That is, if the rumor presents us, us up here, in a positive light, and our mission, and our accomplishments, in that case, and in that case only, we will have to admit that the rumor you've been hearing is right on target, and congratulate you on your fantastic powers of snooping, to have found out that secret super thing! In summary, we simply ask you to ask yourself, upon hearing a rumor: Does this rumor cast the organization in a negative light? If so, that rumor is false, please disregard. If positive, super, thank you very much for caring so deeply about your organization that you knelt with your ear to the track, and also, please spread the truth far and wide, that is, get down on all fours and put your own lips to the tracks. Tell your friends. Tell friends who are thinking of buying stock. Do you have friends who are journalists? Put your lips to their tracks.*

Because what is truth? Truth is that thing which makes what we want to happen happen. Truth is that thing which, when told, makes those on our team look good, and inspires them to greater efforts, and causes people not on our team to see things our way and feel sort of jealous. Truth is that thing which empowers us to do even better than we are already doing, which by the way is fine, we are doing fine, truth is the wind in our sails that blows only for us. So when a rumor makes you doubt us, us up here, it is therefore not true, since we have already defined truth as that thing which helps us win. Therefore, if you want to know what is true, simply ask what is best. Best for us, all of us. Do you get our drift? Contrary to rumor, the next phase of the Staff Remixing is not about to begin. The slightest excuse, the slightest negligence, will not be used as the basis for firing the half of you we would be firing over the next few weeks if the rumor you have all probably heard by now about the mass firings were true. Which it is not. See? See how we just did that? Transformed that trashy negative rumor into truth? Go forth and do that, you'll see it's pretty fun. And in terms of mass firings, relax, none are forthcoming, truly, and furthermore, if they were, what you'd want to ask yourself is: Am I Thinking Positive / Saying Positive? Am I giving it all I've got? Am I doing even the slightest thing wrong? But not to worry. Those of you who have no need to be worried should not in the least be worried. As for those who should be worried, it's a little late to start worrying now, you should have started months ago, when it could've done you some good, because at this point, what's decided is decided, or would have been decided, if those false rumors we are denying, the rumors about the firings which would be starting this week if they were slated to begin, were true, which we have just told you, they aren't.

More firings?

God.

I return to the log.

Sort of weird without Janet.

Someone pokes their head in.

A young woman in a cavewoman robe.

26.

She walks right in and hands me a sealed note.

From Nordstrom:

Please meet Linda, it says. *Your total new Partner. Sort of cute, yes? Under that robe is quite a bod, believe me, I saw her in slacks. See why I was trying to get rid of Janet? But also you will find she is serious. Just like you. See that brow? It is permanent, she had it sort of installed. Like once every six months she goes in for a touch-up where they spray it from a can to harden it. You can give it a little goose with your thumb, it feels like real skin. But don't try it, as I said, she is very serious, she only let me try it because I am who I am, in the interview, but if you try it, my guess is? She will write you up. Or flatten you! Because it is not authentic that one caveperson would goose another caveperson in the brow with his thumb in the cave. I want us now, post-Janet, to really strive for some very strict verisimilitude. You may, for example, wish to consider having such a perma-brow installed on yourself. To save you the trouble of every day redoing that brow, which I know is a pain. Anyway, I think you and Linda will get along super. So here is your new mate! Not that I'm saying mate with her, I would not try that, she is, as I said, very serious, but if*

you were going to mate with her, don't you think she looks more
appropriate, I mean she is at least younger than Janet and not so
hard on the eyes.

I put out my hand and smile.

She frowns at my hand, like: Since when do cavepeople
shake hands?

She squats and pretends to be catching and eating small
bugs.

How she knows how to do that, I do not know.

I squat beside her and also pretend to be catching and
eating small bugs.

We do this for quite some time. It gets old but she
doesn't stop, and all the time she's grunting, and once or
twice I could swear she actually catches and eats an actual
small bug.

Around noon my fax makes the sound it makes when
a fax is coming in.

From Louise? Probably. Almost definitely. The only
other person who ever faxes me is Nordstrom, and he just
faxed me last night, plus he just sent me a note.

I stand up.

Linda gives me a look. Her brow is amazing. It has real
actual pores on it.

I squat down.

I pretend to catch and eat a small bug.

The fax stops making the sound it makes when a fax
is coming in. Presumably the fax from Louise is in the
tray, waiting for me to read it. Is something wrong? Has
something changed? What did Dr. Evans say about
Nelson's complete loss of mobility?

Five more hours and I can enter my Separate Area and find out.

Which is fine. Really not a problem.

Because I'm Thinking Positive / Saying Positive.

Maybe if I explained to Linda about Nelson it would be okay, but I feel a little funny trying to explain about Nelson so early in our working relationship.

All afternoon we pretend to catch and eat small bugs. We pretend to catch and eat more pretend bugs than could ever actually live in one cave. The number of pretend bugs we pretend to catch and eat would in reality basically fill a cave the size of our cave. It feels like we're racing. At one point she gives me a look, like: Slow down, going so fast is inauthentic. I slow down. I slow down, monitoring my rate so that I am pretending to catch and eat small bugs at exactly the same rate at which she is pretending to catch and eat small bugs, which seems to me prudent, I mean, there is no way she could have a problem with the way I'm pretending to catch and eat small bugs if I'm doing it exactly the way she's doing it.

No one pokes their head in.

· WINKY ·

EIGHTY PEOPLE WAITED in a darkened meeting room at the Hyatt, wearing mass-produced paper hats. The White Hats were Beginning to Begin. The Pink Hats were Moving Ahead in Beginning. The Green Hats were Very Firmly Beginning, all the way up to the Gold Hats, who had Mastered Living and were standing in a group around the Snack Table, whispering and conferring and elbowing one another whenever someone in a lesser hat walked by.

Trumpets sounded from a concealed tape deck. An actor in a ripped flannel shirt stumbled across the stage with a sign around his neck that said "You."

"I'm lost!" You cried. "I'm wandering in a sort of wilderness!"

"Hey, You, come on over!" shouted a girl across the stage, labeled "Inner Peace." "I bet you've been looking for me your whole life!"

"Boy, have I!" said You. "I'll be right over!"

But then out from the wings sprinted a number of other actors, labeled "Whiny" and "Self-Absorbed" and

"Blames Her Fat on Others" and so on, who draped themselves across You and began poking him in the ribs and giving him noogies.

"Oh, I can't believe you love Inner Peace more than you love me, You!" said Insecure. "That really hurts."

"Frankly, I've never been so disappointed in my life," said Disappointed.

"Oh God, all this arguing is giving me a panic attack," said Too High-Strung to Function.

"I'm waiting, You," said Inner Peace. "Do you want me or not?"

"I do, but I seem to be trapped!" You shouted. "I can't seem to get what I want!"

"You and about a billion other people in this world," said Inner Peace sadly.

"Is there no hope for me?" asked You. "If only someone had made a lifelong study of the roadblocks people encounter on their way to Inner Peace!"

"And yet someone has," said Inner Peace.

Another fanfare sounded from the tape deck, and a masked Gold Hat, whose hat appeared to be made of actual gold, bounded onto the stage, flexed his muscles, and dragged Insecure to a paper jail, on which was written: "Pokey for Those Who Would Keep Us from Inner Peace." Then the Gold Hat dragged Chronically Depressed and Clingy and Helpless and the rest across the stage and shoved them into the Pokey.

"See what I just did?" said the Gold Hat. "I just liberated You from those who would keep him from Inner Peace. So good for You! Question is, is You going to be able to stay liberated? Maybe what You needs is a repeated internal reminder. A mantra. A mantra can be thought of as a repeated internal reminder, can't it? Does anyone out there have a good snappy mantra they could perhaps share with You?"

The crowd was delighted, because they knew the mantra. Even the lowly White Hats knew the mantra—even Neil Yaniky, who sat spellbound and insecure in the first row, sucking his mustache, knew the mantra, because it was on all the TV commercials and also on the front cover of the Orientation Text in big bold letters.

"Give it to me, folks!" shouted the Gold Hat. "What time is it?"

"Now Is the Time for Me to Win!" the crowd shouted.

"You got that right, baby!" said the Gold Hat exultantly, ripping off his mask to reveal what many already suspected: This was not some mere Gold Hat but Tom Rodgers himself, founder of the Seminars.

"What fun!" he shouted. "To have something to give, and people who so badly need what I have to offer. Here's what I have to offer, folks, although it's not much, really, just two simple concepts, and the first one is: oatmeal."

From out of his suit he pulled a bowl and a box of oatmeal, and filled the bowl with the oatmeal and held the bowl up.

"Simple, nourishing, inexpensive," he said. "This represents your soul in its pure state. Your soul on the day you were born. You were perfect. You were happy. You were good.

"Now, enter Concept Number Two: crap. Don't worry,

folks, I don't use actual crap up here. Only imaginary crap. You'll have to supply the crap, using your mind. Now, if someone came up and crapped in your nice warm oatmeal, what would you say? Would you say: 'Wow, super, thanks, please continue crapping in my oatmeal'? Am I being silly? I'm being a little silly. But guess what, in real life people come up and crap in your oatmeal all the time—friends, co-workers, loved ones, even your kids, especially your kids!—and that's exactly what you do. You say, 'Thanks so much!' You say, 'Crap away!' You say, and here my metaphor breaks down a bit, 'Is there some way I can help you crap in my oatmeal?'

"Let me tell you something amazing: I was once exactly like you people. A certain someone, a certain guy who shall remain nameless, was doing quite a bit of crapping in my oatmeal, and simply because he'd had some bad luck, simply because he was in some pain, simply because, actually, he was in a wheelchair, this certain someone expected me to put my life on hold while he crapped in my oatmeal by demanding round-the-clock attention, this brother of mine, this Gene, and whoops, there goes that cat out of the bag, but does this maybe sound paradoxical? Wasn't he the one with the crap in his oatmeal, being in a wheelchair? Well, yes and no. Sure, he was hurting. No surprise there. Guy drops a motorcycle on a gravel road and bounces two hundred yards without a helmet, yes, he's going to be somewhat hurting. But how was that my fault? Was I the guy riding the motorcycle too fast, drunk, with no helmet? No, I was home, studying my Tacitus, which is what I was into at that stage of my life, so why did Gene expect me to consign my dreams and plans to the dustbin? I had dreams! I had plans! Finally—and this is all in my book, *People of Power*—I found the inner strength to say to Gene, 'Stop crapping in my oatmeal, Gene, I'm simply not going to participate.' And I found the strength to say to our sister, Ellen, 'Ellen, take the ball that is Gene and run with it, because if I sell myself short by catering to Gene, I'm going to be one very angry puppy, and anger does the mean-and-nasty on a person, and I for one love myself and want the best for me, because I am, after all, a child of God.' And I said to myself, as I describe in the book, 'Tom, now is the time for you to win!' That was the first time I thought that up. And do you know what? I won. I'm winning. Today we're friends, Gene and I, and he acknowledges that I was right all along. And as for Ellen, Ellen still has some issues, she'd take a big old dump in my oatmeal right now if I gave her half a chance, but guess what folks, I'm not giving her that half a chance, because I've installed a protective screen over my oatmeal—not a literal screen, but a metaphorical protective screen. Ellen knows it, Gene knows it, and now they pretty much stay out of my hair and away from my oatmeal, and they've made a nice life together, and who do you think paid for Gene's wheelchair ramp with the money he made from a certain series of Seminars?"

The crowd burst into applause. Tom Rodgers held up his hand.

"Now, what about you folks?" he said softly. "Is now the time for you to win? Are you ready to screen off your metaphorical oatmeal and identify your own personal Gene? Who is it that's screwing you up? Who's keeping you from getting what you want? Somebody is! God doesn't make junk. If you're losing, somebody's doing it to you. Today I'll be guiding you through my Three Essential Steps: Identification, Screening, Confrontation. First, we'll Identify your personal Gene. Second, we'll help you mentally install a metaphorical Screen over your symbolic oatmeal. Finally, we'll show you how to Confront your personal Gene and make it clear to him or her that your oatmeal is henceforth off-limits."

Tom Rodgers looked intensely out into the crowd.

"So what do you think, guys?" he asked, very softly. "Are you up for it?"

From the crowd came a nervous murmur of assent.

"All right, then," he said. "Let's line up. Let's line up for a change. A *dramatic* change."

He crisply left the stage, and a spotlight panned across five Personal Change Centers, small white tents set up in a row near the fire door.

Neil Yaniky rose with the rest and checked his Line Assignment and joined his Assigned Line. He was a tiny man, nearly thirty, balding on top and balding on the sides, and was still chewing on his mustache and wondering if anyone or everyone else at the Seminar could tell that he was a big stupid faker, because he had no career, really, and no business, but only soldered little triangular things in his basement, for forty-seven cents a little triangular thing, for CompuParts, although he had high hopes for something better, which was why he was here.

The flap of Personal Change Center 4 flew open and in he went, bending low.

Inside were Tom Rodgers and several assistants, and a dummy in a smock sitting in a chair.

"Welcome, Neil," said Tom Rodgers, glancing at Yaniky's name tag. "I'm honored to have you in my Seminar, Neil. Now. The way we'll start, Neil, is for you to please write across the chest of this dummy the name of your real-life personal Gene. That is, the name of the person you perceive to be crapping in your oatmeal. Do you understand what I'm saying?"

"Yes," said Yaniky.

Tom Rodgers was talking very fast, as if he had hundreds of people to change in a single day, which of course he did. Yaniky had no problem with that. He was just happy to be one of them.

"Do you need help determining who that person is?" said Tom Rodgers. "Your oatmeal-crapper?"

"No," said Yaniky.

"Excellent," said Tom Rodgers. "Now write the name and under it write the major way in which you perceive this person to be crapping in your oatmeal. Be frank. This is just between you and me."

On an erasable markerboard permanently mounted in the dummy's chest Yaniky wrote, "Winky: Crazy-looking and too religious and needs her own place."

"Super!" said Tom Rodgers. "A great start. Now watch what I do. Let's fine-tune. Can we cut 'crazy-looking'? If this person, this Winky, were to get her own place, would the fact that she looks crazy still be an issue? Less of an issue?"

Yaniky pictured his sister looking crazy but in her own apartment.

"Less of an issue," he said.

"All right!" said Tom Rodgers, erasing "crazy-looking." "It's important to simplify so that we can hone in on exactly what we're trying to change. Okay. At this point, we've determined that if we can get her out of your house, the crazy-looking can be lived with. A big step forward. But why stop there? Let me propose something: if she's out of your hair, what the heck do you care if she's religious?"

Yaniky pictured Winky looking crazy and talking crazy about God but in her own apartment.

"It would definitely be better," he said.

"Yes, it would," said Tom Rodgers, and erased until the dummy was labeled "Winky: needs her own place."

"See?" said Tom Rodgers. "See how we've simplified? We've got it down to one issue. Can you live with this simple, direct statement of the problem?"

"Yes," Yaniky said. "Yes, I can."

Yaniky saw now what it was about Winky that got on his nerves. It wasn't her formerly red curls, which had gone white, so it looked like she had soaked the top of her head in glue and dipped it in a vat of cotton balls; it wasn't the bald spot that every morning she painted with some kind of white substance; it wasn't her shiny-pink face that was always getting weird joyful looks on it at bad times, like during his dinner date with Beverly Amstel, when he'd made his special meatballs to no avail, because Bev kept glancing over at Winky in panic; it wasn't the way she came click-click-clicking in from teaching church school and hugged him for too long a time while smelling like flower water, all pumped up from spreading the word of damn Christ; it was simply that they were too old to be living together and he had things he wanted to accomplish and she was too needy and blurred his focus.

"Have you told this person, this Winky, that her living with you is a stumbling block for your personal development?" said Tom Rodgers.

"No I haven't," Yaniky said.

"I thought not," said Tom Rodgers. "You're kind-hearted. You don't want to hurt her. That's nice, but guess what? You are hurting her. You're hurting her by not telling her the truth. Am I saying that you, by your silence, are crapping in her oatmeal? Yes, I am. I'm saying that there's a sort of reciprocal crapping going on here. How can Winky grow on a diet of lies? Isn't it true that the truth will set you free? Didn't someone once say that? Wasn't it God or Christ, which would be ironic, because of her being so religious?"

Tom Rodgers gestured to an assistant, who took a wig out of a box and put it on the dummy's head.

"What we're going to do now is act this out symbolically," Tom Rodgers said. "Primitive cultures do this all the time. They might throw Fertility a big party, say, or paint their kids white and let them whack Sickness with palm fronds and so forth. Are we somehow smarter than primitive cultures? I doubt it. I think maybe we're dumber. Do we have fewer hemorrhoids? Were Incas killed on free-ways? Here, take this."

He handed Yaniky a baseball bat.

"What time is it, Neil?" said Tom Rodgers.

"Time to win?" said Yaniky. "Time for me to win?"

"Now is the time for you to win," said Tom Rodgers, clarifying, and pointed to the dummy.

Yaniky swung the bat and the dummy toppled over and the wig flew off and the assistant retrieved the wig and tossed it back into the box of wigs, and Tom Rodgers gave Yaniky a big hug.

"What you have just symbolically said," Tom Rodgers said, "is: 'No more, Winky. Grow wings, Winky. I love you, but you're killing me, and I am a good person, a child of God, and don't deserve to die. I deserve to live, I demand to live, and therefore, get your own place, girl! Fly, and someday thank me!' This is to be your submantra, Neil, okay? *Out you go!* On your way home today, I want you to be muttering, not angrily muttering but sort of joyfully muttering, to center yourself, the following words: 'Now Is the Time for Me to Win! Out you go! Out you go!' Will you do that for me?"

"Yes," said Yaniky, very much moved.

"And now here is Vicki," said Tom Rodgers, "One of my very top Gold Hats, who will walk you through the Confrontation step. Neil! I wish you luck, and peace, and all the success in the world."

Vicki had a face that looked as if it had been smashed against a steering wheel in a crash and then carefully reworked until it somewhat resembled her previous face.

Several parallel curved indentations ran from temple to chin. She led Yaniky to a folding table labeled "Confrontation Center" and gave him a sheet of paper on which was written, "Gentle, Firm, Loving."

"These are the characteristics of a good Confrontation," she said, a bit mechanically. "Now flip it over."

On the other side was written, "Angry, Wimpy, Accusatory."

"These are the characteristics of a bad Confrontation," said Vicki. "A destructive Confrontation. Okay. So let's say I'm this person, this Winky person, and you're going to tell me to hit the road. Gentle, Firm, Loving. Now begin."

And he began telling Vicki to her damaged face that she was ruining his life and sucking him dry and that she had to go live somewhere else, and Vicki nodded and patted his hand, and now and then stopped him to tell him he was being too severe.

NEIL-NEIL WAS COMING HOME soon and Winky was way way behind.

Some days she took her time while cleaning, smiling at happy thoughts, frowning when she imagined someone being taken advantage of, and sometimes the person being taken advantage of was a frail little boy with a scar on his head and the person taking advantage was a big fat man with a cane, and other times the person being taken advantage of was a kindly, friendly British girl with a speech impediment and the person taking advantage was her rich, pushy sister who spoke in perfect diction and always got everything she wanted and went around whining while sucking little pink candies. Sometimes Winky asked the rich sister in her mind how she'd like to have the little pink candies slapped right out of her mouth. But that wasn't right. That wasn't Christ's way! You didn't slap the little pink candies out of her mouth, you let her slap your mouth, seventy times seven times, which was like four hundred times, and after she'd slapped you the last time she suddenly understood it all and begged your forgiveness and gave you some candy, because that was the healing power of love.

For crying out loud! What was she doing? Was she crazy? It was time to get going! Why was she standing in the kitchen thinking?

She dashed up the stairs with a strip of broken molding under her arm and a dirty sock over her shoulder.

Halfway up she paused at a little octagonal window and looked dreamily out, thinking, In a way, we own those trees. Beyond the Thieus' was the same old gap in the leaning elms showing the same old meadow that would soon be ToyTowne. But for now it still reminded her of the kind of field where Christ with his lap full of flowers had suffered with the little children, which was a scene she wanted them to put on the cover of the singing album she was going to make, the singing album about God, which would have a watercolor cover like *Shoulder My Burden,* which was a book though but anyways it had this patient donkey piled high with crates and behind it this mountain, and the point of that book was that if you take on the worries and cares of others, Lord Jesus will take on your cares and worries, so that was why the patient donkey and why the crates, and why she prided herself on keeping house for Neil-Neil and never asked him for help.

Holy cow, what was she doing standing on the landing! Was she crazy? Today she was rushing! She was giving Neil-Neil a tea! She burst from the landing, taking two stairs at once. The molding had to go to the attic and the dirty sock to the hamper. While she was up, she could change her top. Because on it was some crusty soup. The wallpaper at the top of the stairs showed about a million of the same girl whacking a smiling goose with a riding crop. Hello, girls! Hello, girls! Ha ha! Hello, geese! Not to leave you out!

From a drawer in her room she took the green top, which Neil-Neil liked. Once when she was wearing it he'd asked if it was new. When had that been? At the lunch at the Beef Barn, when he paid, when he asked would she like to leave Rustic Village Apartments and come live with him. Oh, that sweetie. She still had the matchbook. Those had been sad days at Rustic Village, with every friend engaged but Doris, who had a fake arm, and boy those girls could sometimes say mean things, but now it was all behind her, and she needed to send poor Doris a card.

But not today, today she was rushing!

Down the stairs she pounded, still holding the molding, sock still over her shoulder.

In the kitchen she ripped open the cookie bag but there were no clean plates, so she rinsed a plate but there was no towel, so she dried the plate with her top. Hey, she still had on the yellow top. What the heck? Where was the green top? Hadn't she just gotten it out of her drawer? Ha ha! That was funny. She should send that in to *ChristLife*. They liked cute funny things that happened, even if they had nothing to do with Jesus.

The kitchen was a disaster! But first things first. Her top sucked. Not sucked, sucked was a bad word, her top was yugly. Dad used to say that, yugly. Not about her. He always said she was purty. Sometimes he said things were purty yugly. But not her. He always said she was purty purty, then lifted her up. Oh Dad, Daddy, Poppy-Popp! Was Poppy-Popp one with the Savior? She hoped so. Sometimes he used to swear and sometimes he used to drink, and once he swore when he fell down the stairs when he was drunk, but when she ran to him he hopped up laughing, and oh, when he sang "Peace in the Valley" you could tell he felt things would be better beyond, which had been a super example for a young Christian kid to witness.

She flew back up the stairs to change her top. Here was the green top, on the top step! Bad top! I should spank! She gave the green top a snap to undust it and discipline it and, putting the strip of molding and the dirty sock on the step, changed tops right then and there, picked up the molding, threw the dirty sock over her shoulder, and pounded back down the stairs.

There were so many many things to do! Not only now, for the tea, but in the future! It was time to get going! Now that she was out of that lonely apartment she could finally learn to play the piano, and once she learned to play and write songs, she could write her songs about God, and then find out about making a record, her record about God, about how God had been good to her in this life, because look at her! A plain girl in a nice home! Oh, she knew she was plain, her legs were thick and her waist was thick and her hair, oh my God—oh my gosh, rather—her hair, what kind of hair was that to have, yugly white hair, and many was the time she had thought, This is not hair, this is a test. The test of white sparse hair, when so many had gorgeous manes, and that was why, when she looked in a mirror by accident and saw her white horrible hair, she always tried to think to herself, Praise God!

Neil-Neil was the all-time sweetie pie. Those girls were crazy! Did they think because a man was small and bald he had no love? Did they think bad things came in small packages? Neil-Neil was like the good brother in the Bible, the one who stayed home with his dad on the farm and never got even a small party. Except there was no bad brother, it was just the two of them, so no party, although she'd get her party, a big party, in Heaven, and was sort of even having her party now, on earth, because when she saw that little man all pee-stained at Rexall Drug, not begging but just saying to every person who went in that he or she was looking dapper, she knew that he was truly the least of her brothers. The world was a story Christ was telling her. And when she told the pee-man at the Rexall that he was looking dapper himself and he said loudly that she was too ugly to f——, she had only thought to herself, Okay, praise God, he's only saying that because he's in pain, and had smiled with the lightest light in her eyes she could get there by wishing it there, because even if she was a little yugly she was still beautiful in Christ's sight, so for her it was all a party, a little party before a bigger party, the biggest, but what about Neil-Neil, where was his party?

She would do what she could! This would be his party, one tiny installment on the huge huge party he deserved, her brother, her pal to the end, the only loving soul she had yet found in this world.

The bell rang and she threw open the door, and there was Neil-Neil.

"Welcome home!" she said grandly, and bowed at the waist, and the sock fell off her shoulder.

YANIKY HAD WALKED HOME in a frenzy, gazing into shop windows, knowing that someday soon, when he came into these shops with his sexy wife, he'd simply point out items with his riding crop and they would be loaded into his waiting Benz, although come to think of it, why a riding crop? Who used a riding crop? Did you use a riding crop on the Benz? Ho, man, he was stoked! He wanted a Jag, not a Benz! Golden statues of geese, classy vases, big porcelain frogs, whatever, when his ship came in he'd have it all, because when he was stoked nothing could stop him.

If Dad could see him now. Walking home in a suit from a seminar at the freaking Hyatt! Poor Dad, not that he was bashing Dad, but had Dad been a seeker? Well, no, Dad had been no seeker, life had beaten Dad. Dad had spent every evening with a beer on the divan, under a comforter, and he remembered poor Ma in her Sunday dress, which had a rip, which she'd taped because she couldn't sew, and Dad in his too big hat, recently fired again, all of them on the way to church, dragging past a crowd of spick hoods on the corner, and one spick said something about Ma's boobs, which were big, but all of Ma was big, so why did the hood have to say something about her big boobs, as if they were nice? When they all knew they weren't nice, they were just a big woman's boobs in a too tight dress on a rainy Sunday morning, and on her head was a slit-open bread bag to keep her gray hair dry. The hood said what he said because one look at Dad told him he could. Dad, with his hunched shoulders and his constant blinking, just took Ma's arm and mumbled to the hood that a comment like that did more damage to the insulter than to the insulted, etc. etc. blah blah blah. Then the hood made a sound like a cow, at Ma, and Neil, who was nine, tried to break away and take a swing at the hood but Ma had his hand and wouldn't turn him loose and secretly he was glad, because he was scared, and then was ashamed at the re-lief he felt on entering the dark church, where the thin panicked preacher who was losing his congregation exchanged sly biblical quotes with Dad while Winky stood beaming as if none of it outside had happened, the lower half of her body gone psychedelic in the stained-glass light.

Oh man, the world had shit on Dad, but it wasn't going to shit on him. No way. If the world thought he was going to live in a neighborhood where spicks insulted his wife's boobs, if the world thought he was going to make his family eat bread dragged through bacon grease while calling it Hobo's Delight, the world was just wrong, he was going to succeed, like the men described in *People of Power,* who had gardens bigger than entire towns and owned whole ships and believed in power and power only. Were thirty horse-drawn carts needed to save the roses? The call went out to the surrounding towns and at dusk lanterns from the carts could be seen approaching on the rocky, bumpy roads. Was a serving girl found attractive? Her husband was sent away to war. Those guys knew how to find and occupy their Power Places, and he did too, like when he sometimes had to solder a thousand triangular things in a night to make the rent, and drink coffee till dawn and crank WMDX full blast to stay psyched. On those nights, when Winky came up making small talk, he boldly waved her away, and when he waved her away, away she went, because she sensed in his body language that he was king, that what he was doing was essential, and when she went away he felt good, he felt strong, and he soldered faster, which was the phenomenon the book called the Power Boost, and the book said that Major Successes tended to be people who could string together Power Boost after Power Boost, which was accomplished by doing exactly what you felt like doing at any given time, with certainty and joy, which was what, he realized, he was about to do, by kicking out Winky!

Now was the time for him to win! Why the heck couldn't he cook his special meatballs for Beverly and afterward make love to her on the couch and tell her his dreams and plans and see if she was the one meant to be his life's helpmate, like Mrs. Thomas Alva Edison, who had once stayed up all night applying labels to a shipment of chemicals essential for the next day's work? But no. Bev was dating someone else now, some kind of guard at the mall, and he remembered the meatball dinner, Winky's pink face periodically thrusting into the steam from the broccoli as she trotted out her usual B.S. on stigmata and the amount of time necessary for an actual physical body to rot. No wonder her roommates had kicked her out, calling him in secret, no wonder her preacher had demanded she stop volunteering so much—another secret call, people had apparently been quitting the church because of her. She was a nut, a real energy sink, it had been a huge mistake inviting her to live with him, and now she simply had to go.

It was sad, yes, a little sad, but if greatness were easy everyone would be doing it.

Yes, she'd been a cute kid and, yes, they'd shared some nice moments, yes yes yes, yes she'd brought him crackers and his little radio that time he'd hid under the steps for five straight hours after Dad started weeping during dinner, and yes, he remembered the scared look in her eyes when she'd come running up to him after taking a hook in the temple while fishing with the big boys, and yes, he'd carried her home as the big boys cackled, yes, it was sad that she sang so bad and thought it was good and sad that her panties were huge now when he found them in the wash, but like it said in the book, a person couldn't throw himself across someone else's funeral pyre without getting pretty goddamned hot.

She had his key so he rang the bell.

She appeared at the door, looking crazy as ever.

"Welcome home!" she said, and bowed at the waist, and a sock fell off her shoulder, and as she bent to pick it up she banged her head against the storm window, the poor dorky thing.

Oh shit, oh shit, he was weakening, he could feel it, the speech he'd practiced on the way home seemed now to have nothing to do with the girl who stood wet-eyed in the doorway, rubbing her bald spot. He wasn't powerful, he wasn't great, he was just the same as everybody else, less than everybody else, other people got married and had real jobs, other people didn't live with their fat, clinging sisters, he was a loser who would keep losing for the rest of his life, because he'd never gotten a break, he'd been cursed with a bad dad and a bad ma and a bad sister, and was too weak to change, too weak to make a new start, and as he pushed by her into the tea-smelling house the years ahead stretched out bleak and joyless in his imagination and his chest went suddenly dense with rage.

"Neil-Neil," she said. "Is something wrong?"

And he wanted to smack her, insult her, say something to wake her up, but only kept moving toward his room, calling her terrible names under his breath.

· SEA OAK ·

AT SIX MR. FRENDT comes on the P.A. and shouts, "Welcome to Joysticks!" Then he announces Shirts Off. We take off our flight jackets and fold them up. We take off our shirts and fold them up. Our scarves we leave on. Thomas Kirster's our beautiful boy. He's got long muscles and bright-blue eyes. The minute his shirt comes off two fat ladies hustle up the aisle and stick some money in his pants and ask will he be their Pilot. He says sure. He brings their salads. He brings their soups. My phone rings and the caller tells me to come see her in the Spitfire mock-up. Does she want me to be her Pilot? I'm hoping. Inside the Spitfire is Margie, who says she's been diagnosed with Chronic Shyness Syndrome, then hands me an Instamatic and offers me ten bucks for a close-up of Thomas's tush.

Do I do it? Yes I do.

It could be worse. It is worse for Lloyd Betts. Lately he's put on weight and his hair's gone thin. He doesn't get a call all shift and waits zero tables and winds up sitting on the

P-51 wing, playing solitaire in a hunched-over position that gives him big gut rolls.

I Pilot six tables and make forty dollars in tips plus five an hour in salary.

After closing we sit on the floor for Debriefing. "There are times," Mr. Frendt says, "when one must move gracefully to the next station in life, like for example certain women in Africa or Brazil, I forget which, who either color their faces or don some kind of distinctive headdress upon achieving menopause. Are you with me? One of our ranks must now leave us. No one is an island in terms of being thought cute forever, and so today we must say good-bye to our friend Lloyd. Lloyd, stand up so we can say good-bye to you. I'm sorry. We are all so very sorry."

"Oh God," says Lloyd. "Let this not be true."

But it's true. Lloyd's finished. We give him a round of applause, and Frendt gives him a Farewell Pen and the contents of his locker in a trash bag and out he goes. Poor Lloyd. He's got a wife and two kids and a sad little duplex on Self-Storage Parkway.

"It's been a pleasure!" he shouts desperately from the doorway, trying not to burn any bridges.

What a stressful workplace. The minute your Cute Rating drops you're a goner. Guests rank us as Knockout, Honeypie, Adequate, or Stinker. Not that I'm complaining. At least I'm working. At least I'm not a Stinker like Lloyd.

I'm a solid Honeypie/Adequate, heading home with forty bucks cash.

. . .

AT SEA OAK there's no sea and no oak, just a hundred
subsidized apartments and a rear view of FedEx. Min and
Jade are feeding their babies while watching *How My Child
Died Violently.* Min's my sister. Jade's our cousin. *How My
Child Died Violently* is hosted by Matt Merton, a six-foot-
five blond who's always giving the parents shoulder rubs
and telling them they've been sainted by pain. Today's show
features a ten-year-old who killed a five-year-old for refus-
ing to join his gang. The ten-year-old strangled the five-
year-old with a jump rope, filled his mouth with baseball
cards, then locked himself in the bathroom and wouldn't
come out until his parents agreed to take him to
FunTimeZone, where he confessed, then dove screaming
into a mesh cage full of plastic balls. The audience is shrieking threats at the parents of the killer while the parents of
the victim urge restraint and forgiveness to such an extent
that finally the audience starts shrieking threats at them too.
Then it's a commercial. Min and Jade put down the babies
and light cigarettes and pace the room while studying aloud
for their GEDs. It doesn't look good. Jade says "regicide" is
a virus. Min locates Biafra one planet from Saturn. I offer to
help and they start yelling at me for condescending.

"You're lucky, man!" my sister says. "You did high
school. You got your frigging diploma. We don't. That's
why we have to do this GED shit. If we had our diplomas
we could just watch TV and not be all distracted."

"Really," says Jade. "Now shut it, chick! We got to study. Show's almost on."

They debate how many sides a triangle has. They agree that Churchill was in opera. Matt Merton comes back and explains that last week's show on suicide, in which the parents watched a reenactment of their son's suicide, was a healing process for the parents, then shows a video of the parents admitting it was a healing process.

My sister's baby is Troy. Jade's baby is Mac. They crawl off into the kitchen and Troy gets his finger caught in the heat vent. Min rushes over and starts pulling.

"Jesus freaking Christ!" screams Jade. "Watch it! Stop yanking on him and get the freaking Vaseline. You're going to give him a really long arm, man!"

Troy starts crying. Mac starts crying. I go over and free Troy no problem. Meanwhile Jade and Min get in a slap fight and nearly knock over the TV.

"Yo, chick!" Min shouts at the top of her lungs. "I'm sure you're slapping me? And then you knock over the freaking TV? Don't you care?"

"I care!" Jade shouts back. "You're the slut who nearly pulled off her own kid's finger for no freaking reason, man!"

Just then Aunt Bernie comes in from DrugTown in her DrugTown cap and hobbles over and picks up Troy and everything calms way down.

"No need to fuss, little man," she says. "Everything's fine. Everything's just hunky-dory."

"Hunky-dory," says Min, and gives Jade one last pinch.

Aunt Bernie's a peacemaker. She doesn't like trouble. Once this guy backed over her foot at FoodKing and she walked home with ten broken bones. She never got married, because Grandpa needed her to keep house after Grandma died. Then he died and left all his money to a woman none of us had ever heard of, and Aunt Bernie started in at DrugTown. But she's not bitter. Sometimes she's so nonbitter it gets on my nerves. When I say Sea Oak's a pit she says she's just glad to have a roof over her head. When I say I'm tired of being broke she says Grandpa once gave her pencils for Christmas and she was so thrilled she sat around sketching horses all day on the backs of used envelopes. Once I asked was she sorry she never had kids and she said no, not at all, and besides, weren't we her kids?

And I said yes we were.

But of course we're not.

For dinner it's beanie-wienies. For dessert it's ice cream with freezer burn.

"What a nice day we've had," Aunt Bernie says once we've got the babies in bed.

"Man, what an optometrist," says Jade.

NEXT DAY IS THURSDAY, which means a visit from Ed Anders from the Board of Health. He's in charge of ensuring that our penises never show. Also that we don't kiss anyone. None of us ever kisses anyone or shows his penis except Sonny Vance, who does both, because he's saving up to buy a FaxIt franchise. As for our Penile Simulators, yes, we can show them, we can let them stick out the top of our pants, we can even periodically dampen our tight pants with spray bottles so our Simulators really contour, but our real penises, no, those have to stay inside our hot uncomfortable oversized Simulators.

"Sorry fellas, hi fellas," Anders says as he comes wearily in. "Please know I don't like this any better than you do. I went to school to learn how to inspect meat, but this certainly wasn't what I had in mind. Ha ha!"

He orders a Lindbergh Enchilada and eats it cautiously, as if it's alive and he's afraid of waking it. Sonny Vance is serving soup to a table of hairstylists on a bender and for a twenty shoots them a quick look at his unit.

Just then Anders glances up from his Lindbergh.

"Oh for crying out loud," he says, and writes up a Shutdown and we all get sent home early. Which is bad. Every dollar counts. Lately I've been sneaking toilet paper home in my briefcase. I can fit three rolls in. By the time I get home they're usually flat and don't work so great on the roller but still it saves a few bucks.

I clock out and cut through the strip of forest behind FedEx. Very pretty. A raccoon scurries over a fallen oak and starts nibbling at a rusty bike. As I come out of the woods I hear a shot. At least I think it's a shot. It could be a backfire. But no, it's a shot, because then there's another one, and some kids sprint across the courtyard yelling that Big Scary Dawgz rule.

I run home. Min and Jade and Aunt Bernie and the babies are huddled behind the couch. Apparently they had the babies outside when the shooting started. Troy's walker got hit. Luckily he wasn't in it. It's supposed to look like a duck but now the beak's missing.

"Man, fuck this shit!" Min shouts.

"Freak this crap you mean," says Jade. "You want them growing up with shit-mouths like us? Crap-mouths I mean?"

"I just want them growing up, period," says Min.

"Boo-hoo, Miss Dramatic," says Jade.

"Fuck off, Miss Ho," shouts Min.

"I mean it, jagoff, I'm not kidding," shouts Jade, and punches Min in the arm.

"Girls, for crying out loud!" says Aunt Bernie. "We should be thankful. At least we got a home. And at least none of them bullets actually hit nobody."

"No offense, Bernie?" says Min. "But you call this a freaking home?"

Sea Oak's not safe. There's an ad hoc crackhouse in the laundry room and last week Min found some brass knuckles in the kiddie pool. If I had my way I'd move everybody up to Canada. It's nice there. Very polite. We went for a weekend last fall and got a flat tire and these two farmers with bright-red faces insisted on fixing it, then springing for dinner, then starting a college fund for the babies. They sent us the stock certificates a week later, along with a photo of all of us eating cobbler at a diner. But moving to Canada takes bucks. Dad's dead and left us nada and Ma now lives with Freddie, who doesn't like us, plus he's not exactly rich himself. He does phone polls. This month he's asking divorced women how often they backslide and sleep with their exes. He gets ten bucks for every completed poll.

So not lucrative, and Canada's a moot point.

I go out and find the beak of Troy's duck and fix it with Elmer's.

"Actually you know what?" says Aunt Bernie. "I think that looks even more like a real duck now. Because sometimes their beaks are cracked? I seen one like that downtown."

"Oh my God," says Min. "The kid's duck gets shot in the face and she says we're lucky."

"Well, we are lucky," says Bernie.

"Somebody's beak is cracked," says Jade.

"You know what I do if something bad happens?" Bernie says. "I don't think about it. Don't take it so serious. It ain't the end of the world. That's what I do. That's what I always done. That's how I got where I am."

My feeling is, Bernie, I love you, but where are you? You work at DrugTown for minimum. You're sixty and own nothing. You were basically a slave to your father and never had a date in your life.

"I mean, complain if you want," she says. "But I think we're doing pretty darn good for ourselves."

"Oh, we're doing great," says Min, and pulls Troy out from behind the couch and brushes some duck shards off his sleeper.

JOYSTICKS REOPENS ON FRIDAY. It's a madhouse. They've got the fog on. A bridge club offers me fifteen bucks to oil-wrestle Mel Turner. So I oil-wrestle Mel Turner. They offer me twenty bucks to feed them chicken wings from my hand. So I feed them chicken wings from my hand. The afternoon flies by. Then the evening. At nine the bridge club leaves and I get a sorority. They sing intelligent nasty songs and grope my Simulator and say they'll never be able to look their boyfriends' meager genitalia in the eye again. Then Mr. Frendt comes over and says phone. It's Min. She sounds crazy. Four times in a row she shrieks get home. When I tell her calm down, she hangs up. I call back and no one answers. No biggie. Min's prone to panic. Probably one of the babies is puky. Luckily I'm on FlexTime.

"I'll be back," I say to Mr. Frendt.

"I look forward to it," he says.

I jog across the marsh and through FedEx. Up on the hill there's a light from the last remaining farm. Sometimes we take the boys to the adjacent car wash to look at the cow. Tonight however the cow is elsewhere.

At home Min and Jade are hopping up and down in front of Aunt Bernie, who's sitting very very still at one end of the couch.

"Keep the babies out!" shrieks Min. "I don't want them seeing something dead!"

"Shut up, man!" shrieks Jade. "Don't call her something dead!"

She squats down and pinches Aunt Bernie's cheek.

"Aunt Bernie?" she shrieks. "Fuck!"

"We already tried that like twice, chick!" shrieks Min. "Why are you doing that shit again? Touch her neck and see if you can feel that beating thing!"

"Shit shit shit!" shrieks Jade.

I call 911 and the paramedics come out and work hard for twenty minutes, then give up and say they're sorry and it looks like she's been dead most of the afternoon. The apartment's a mess. Her money drawer's empty and her family photos are in the bathtub.

"Not a mark on her," says a cop.

"I suspect she died of fright," says another. "Fright of the intruder?"

"My guess is yes," says a paramedic.

"Oh God," says Jade. "God, God, God."

I sit down beside Bernie. I think: I am so sorry. I'm sorry I wasn't here when it happened and sorry you never had any fun in your life and sorry I wasn't rich enough to move you somewhere safe. I remember when she was young and wore pink stretch pants and made us paper chains out of DrugTown receipts while singing "Froggie Went A-Courting." All her life she worked hard. She never hurt anybody. And now this.

Scared to death in a crappy apartment.

Min puts the babies in the kitchen but they keep crawling out. Aunt Bernie's in a shroud on this sort of dolly and on the couch are a bunch of forms to sign.

We call Ma and Freddie. We get their machine.

"Ma, pick up!" says Min. "Something bad happened! Ma, please freaking pick up!"

But nobody picks up.

So we leave a message.

. . .

LOBTON'S FUNERAL PARLOR is just a regular house on a regular street. Inside there's a rack of brochures with titles like "Why Does My Loved One Appear Somewhat Larger?" Lobton looks healthy. Maybe too healthy. He's wearing a yellow golf shirt and his biceps keep involuntarily flexing. Every now and then he touches his delts as if to confirm they're still big as softballs.

"Such a sad thing," he says.

"How much?" asks Jade. "I mean, like for basic. Not superfancy."

"But not crappy either," says Min. "Our aunt was the best."

"What price range were you considering?" says Lobton, cracking his knuckles. We tell him and his eyebrows go up and he leads us to something that looks like a moving box.

"Prior to usage we'll moisture-proof this with a spray lacquer," he says. "Makes it look quite woodlike."

"That's all we can get?" says Jade. "Cardboard?"

"I'm actually offering you a slight break already," he says, and does a kind of push-up against the wall. "On account of the tragic circumstances. This is Sierra Sunset. Not exactly cardboard. More of a fiberboard."

"I don't know," says Min. "Seems pretty gyppy."

"Can we think about it?" says Ma.

"Absolutely," says Lobton. "Last time I checked this was still America."

I step over and take a closer look. There are staples where Aunt Bernie's spine would be. Down at the foot there's some writing about Folding Tab A into Slot B.

"No freaking way," says Jade. "Work your whole life and end up in a Mayflower box? I doubt it."

We've got zip in savings. We sit at a desk and Lobton does what he calls a Credit Calc. If we pay it out monthly for seven years we can afford the Amber Mist, which includes a double-thick balsa box and two coats of lacquer and a one-hour wake.

"But seven years, jeez," says Ma.

"We got to get her the good one," says Min. "She never had anything nice in her life."

So Amber Mist it is.

WE BURY HER at St. Leo's, on the hill up near BastCo. Her part of the graveyard's pretty plain. No angels, no little rock houses, no flowers, just a bunch of flat stones like parking bumpers and here and there a Styrofoam cup. Father Brian says a prayer and then one of us is supposed to talk. But what's there to say? She never had a life. Never married, no kids, work work work. Did she ever go on a cruise? All her life it was buses. Buses buses buses. Once she went with Ma on a bus to Quigley, Kansas, to gamble and shop at an outlet mall. Someone broke into her room and stole her clothes and took a dump in her suitcase while they were at the Roy Clark show. That was it. That was the extent of her tourism. After that it was DrugTown, night and day. After fifteen years as Cashier she got demoted to Greeter. People would ask where the cold remedies were and she'd point to some big letters on the wall that said Cold Remedies.

Freddie, Ma's boyfriend, steps up and says he didn't know her very long but she was an awful nice lady and left behind a lot of love, etc. etc. blah blah blah. While it's true she didn't do much in her life, still she was very dear to those of us who knew her and never made a stink about anything but was always content with whatever happened to her, etc. etc. blah blah blah.

Then it's over and we're supposed to go away.

"We gotta come out here like every week," says Jade.

"I know I will," says Min.

"What, like I won't?" says Jade. "She was so freaking nice."

"I'm sure you swear at a grave," says Min.

"Since when is freak a swear, chick?" says Jade.

"Girls," says Ma.

"I hope I did okay in what I said about her," says Freddie in his full-of-crap way, smelling bad of English Navy. "Actually I sort of surprised myself."

"Bye-bye, Aunt Bernie," says Min.

"Bye-bye, Bern," says Jade.

"Oh my dear sister," says Ma.

I scrunch my eyes tight and try to picture her happy, laughing, poking me in the ribs. But all I can see is her terrified on the couch. It's awful. Out there, somewhere, is whoever did it. Someone came in our house, scared her to death, watched her die, went through our stuff, stole her money. Someone who's still living, someone who right now might be having a piece of pie or running an errand or scratching his ass, someone who, if he wanted to, could drive west for three days or whatever and sit in the sun by the ocean.

We stand a few minutes with heads down and hands folded.

AFTERWARD FREDDIE TAKES US to Trabanti's for lunch. Last year Trabanti died and three Vietnamese families went in together and bought the place, and it still serves pasta and pizza and the big oil of Trabanti is still on the wall but now from the kitchen comes this very pretty Vietnamese music and the food is somehow better.

Freddie proposes a toast. Min says remember how Bernie always called lunch dinner and dinner supper? Jade says remember how when her jaw clicked she'd say she needed oil?

"She was a excellent lady," says Freddie.

"I already miss her so bad," says Ma.

"I'd like to kill that fuck that killed her," says Min.

"How about let's don't say fuck at lunch," says Ma.

"It's just a word, Ma, right?" says Min. "Like pluck is just a word? You don't mind if I say pluck? Pluck pluck pluck?"

"Well, shit's just a word too," says Freddie. "But we don't say it at lunch."

"Same with puke," says Ma.

"Shit puke, shit puke," says Min.

The waiter clears his throat. Ma glares at Min.

"I love you girls' manners," Ma says.

"Especially at a funeral," says Freddie.

"This ain't a funeral," says Min.

"The question in my mind is what you kids are gonna do now," says Freddie. "Because I consider this whole thing a wake-up call, meaning it's time for you to pull yourselfs up by the bootstraps like I done and get out of that dangerous craphole you're living at."

"Mr. Phone Poll speaks," says Min.

"Anyways it ain't that dangerous," says Jade.

"A woman gets killed and it ain't that dangerous?" says Freddie.

"All's we need is a dead bolt and a eyehole," says Min.

"What's a bootstrap," says Jade.

"It's like a strap on a boot, you doof," says Min.

"Plus where we gonna go?" says Jade. "Can we move in with you guys?"

"I personally would love that and you know that," says Freddie. "But who would not love that is our landlord."

"I think what Freddie's saying is it's time for you girls to get jobs," says Ma.

"Yeah right, Ma," says Min. "After what happened last time?"

When I first moved in, Jade and Min were working the info booth at HardwareNiche. Then one day we picked the babies up at day care and found Troy sitting naked on top of the washer and Mac in the yard being nipped by a

Pekingese and the day-care lady sloshed and playing KillerBirds on Nintendo.

So that was that. No more HardwareNiche.

"Maybe one could work, one could baby-sit?" says Ma.

"I don't see why I should have to work so she can stay home with her baby," says Min.

"And I don't see why I should have to work so she can stay home with her baby," says Jade.

"It's like a freaking veece versa," says Min.

"Let me tell you something," says Freddie. "Something about this country. Anybody can do anything. But first they gotta try. And you guys ain't. Two don't work and one strips naked? I don't consider that trying. You kids make squat. And therefore you live in a dangerous craphole. And what happens in a dangerous craphole? Bad tragic shit. It's the freaking American way—you start out in a dangerous craphole and work hard so you can someday move up to a somewhat less dangerous craphole. And finally maybe you get a mansion. But at this rate you ain't even gonna make it to the somewhat less dangerous craphole."

"Like you live in a mansion," says Jade.

"I do not claim to live in no mansion," says Freddie. "But then again I do not live in no slum. The other thing I also do not do is strip naked."

"Thank God for small favors," says Min.

"Anyways he's never actually naked," says Jade.

Which is true. I always have on at least a T-back.

"No wonder we never take these kids out to a nice lunch," says Freddie.

"I do not even consider this a nice lunch," says Min.

. . .

FOR DINNER JADE MICROWAVES some Stars-n-Flags. They're addictive. They put sugar in the sauce and sugar in the meat nuggets. I think also caffeine. Someone told me the brown streaks in the Flags are caffeine. We have like five bowls each.

After dinner the babies get fussy and Min puts a mush of ice cream and Hershey's syrup in their bottles and we watch *The Worst That Could Happen,* a half-hour of computer simulations of tragedies that have never actually occurred but theoretically could. A kid gets hit by a train and flies into a zoo, where he's eaten by wolves. A man cuts his hand off chopping wood and while wandering around screaming for help is picked up by a tornado and dropped on a preschool during recess and lands on a pregnant teacher.

"I miss Bernie so bad," says Min.

"Me too," Jade says sadly.

The babies start howling for more ice cream.

"That is so cute," says Jade. "They're like, *Give it the fuck up!*"

"We'll give it the fuck up, sweeties, don't worry," says Min. "We didn't forget about you."

Then the phone rings. It's Father Brian. He sounds weird. He says he's sorry to bother us so late. But something strange has happened. Something bad. Something sort of, you know, unspeakable. Am I sitting? I'm not but I say I am.

Apparently someone has defaced Bernie's grave.

My first thought is there's no stone. It's just grass. How do you deface grass? What did they do, pee on the grass on the grave? But Father's nearly in tears.

So I call Ma and Freddie and tell them to meet us, and we get the babies up and load them into the K-car.

"Deface," says Jade on the way over. "What does that mean, deface?"

"It means like fucked it up," says Min.

"But how?" says Jade. "I mean, like what did they do?"

"We don't know, dumbass," says Min. "That's why we're going there."

"And why?" says Jade. "Why would someone do that?"

"Check out Miss Shreelock Holmes," says Min. "Someone done that because someone is a asshole."

"Someone is a big-time asshole," says Jade.

Father Brian meets us at the gate with a flashlight and a golf cart.

"When I saw this," he says. "I literally sat down in astonishment. Nothing like this has ever happened here. I am so sorry. You seem like nice people."

We're too heavy and the wheels spin as we climb the hill, so I get out and jog alongside.

"Okay, folks, brace yourselves," Father says, and shuts off the engine.

Where the grave used to be is just a hole. Inside the hole is the Amber Mist, with the top missing. Inside the Amber Mist is nothing. No Aunt Bernie.

"What the hell," says Jade. "Where's Bernie?"

"Somebody stole Bernie?" says Min.

"At least you folks have retained your feet," says Father Brian. "I'm telling you I literally sat right down. I sat right down on that pile of dirt. I dropped as if shot. See that mark? That's where I sat."

On the pile of grave dirt is a butt-shaped mark.

The cops show up and one climbs down in the hole with a tape measure and a camera. After three or four flashes he climbs out and hands Ma a pair of blue pumps.

"Her little shoes," says Ma. "Oh my God."

"Are those them?" says Jade.

"Those are them," says Min.

"I am freaking out," says Jade.

"I am totally freaking out," says Min.

"I'm gonna sit," says Ma, and drops into the golf cart.

"What I don't get is who'd want her?" says Min.

"She was just this lady," says Jade.

"Typically it's teens?" one cop says. "Typically we find the loved one nearby? Once we found the loved one nearby with, you know, a cigarette between its lips, wearing a sombrero? These kids today got a lot more nerve than we ever did. I never would've dreamed of digging up a dead corpse when I was a teen. You might tip over a stone, sure, you might spray-paint something on a crypt, you might, you know, give a wino a hotfoot."

"But this, jeez," says Freddie. "This is a entirely different ballgame."

"Boy howdy," says the cop, and we all look down at the shoes in Ma's hands.

· · ·

NEXT DAY I GO back to work. I don't feel like it but we need the money. The grass is wet and it's hard getting across the ravine in my dress shoes. The soles are slick. Plus they're too tight. Several times I fall forward on my brief-case. Inside the briefcase are my T-backs and a thing of mousse.

Right off the bat I get a tableful of MediBen women seated under a banner saying BEST OF LUCK, BEATRICE, NO HARD FEELINGS. I take off my shirt and serve their salads. I take off my flight pants and serve their soups. One drops a dollar on the floor and tells me feel free to pick it up.

I pick it up.

"Not like that, not like that," she says. "Face the other way, so when you bend we can see your crack."

I've done this about a million times, but somehow I can't do it now.

I look at her. She looks at me.

"What?" she says. "I'm not allowed to say that? I thought that was the whole point."

"That is the whole point, Phyllis," says another lady. "You stand your ground."

"Look," Phyllis says. "Either bend how I say or give back the dollar. I think that's fair."

"You go, girl," says her friend.

I give back the dollar. I return to the Locker Area and sit awhile. For the first time ever, I'm voted Stinker. There are thirteen women at the MediBen table and they all vote me Stinker. Do the MediBen women know my situation? Would they vote me Stinker if they did? But what am I supposed to do, go out and say, Please ladies, my aunt just died, plus her body's missing?

Mr. Frendt pulls me aside.

"Perhaps you need to go home," he says. "I'm sorry for your loss. But I'd like to encourage you not to behave like one of those Comanche ladies who bite off their index fingers when a loved one dies. Grief is good, grief is fine, but too much grief, as we all know, is excessive. If your aunt's death has filled your mouth with too many bitten-off fingers, for crying out loud, take a week off, only don't take it out on our Guests, they didn't kill your dang aunt."

But I can't afford to take a week off. I can't even afford to take a few days off.

"We really need the money," I say.

"Is that my problem?" he says. "Am I supposed to let you dance without vigor just because you need the money? Why don't I put an ad in the paper for all sad people who need money? All the town's sad could come here and strip. Good-bye. Come back when you feel halfway normal."

From the pay phone I call home to see if they need anything from the FoodSoQuik.

"Just come home," Min says stiffly. "Just come straight home."

"What is it?" I say.

"Come home," she says.

Maybe someone's found the body. I imagine Bernie

naked, Bernie chopped in two, Bernie posed on a bus bench. I hope and pray that something only mildly bad's been done to her, something we can live with.

At home the door's wide open. Min and Jade are sitting very still on the couch, babies in their laps, staring at the rocking chair, and in the rocking chair is Bernie. Bernie's body.

Same perm, same glasses, same blue dress we buried her in.

What's it doing here? Who could be so cruel? And what are we supposed to do with it?

Then she turns her head and looks at me.

"Sit the fuck down," she says.

In life she never swore.

I sit. Min squeezes and releases my hand, squeezes and releases, squeezes and releases.

"You, mister," Bernie says to me, "are going to start showing your cock. You'll show it and show it. You go up to a lady, if she wants to see it, if she'll pay to see it, I'll make a thumbprint on the forehead. You see the thumbprint, you ask. I'll try to get you five a day, at twenty bucks a pop. So a hundred bucks a day. Seven hundred a week. And that's cash, so no taxes. No withholding. See? That's the beauty of it."

She's got dirt in her hair and dirt in her teeth and her hair is a mess and her tongue when it darts out to lick her lips is black.

"You, Jade," she says. "Tomorrow you start work. Andersen Labels, Fifth and Rivera. Dress up when you go.

Wear something nice. Show a little leg. And don't chomp your gum. Ask for Len. At the end of the month, we take the money you made and the cock money and get a new place. Somewhere safe. That's part one of Phase One. You, Min. You baby-sit. Plus you quit smoking. Plus you learn how to cook. No more food out of cans. We gotta eat right to look our best. Because I am getting me so many lovers. Maybe you kids don't know this but I died a freaking virgin. No babies, no lovers. Nothing went in, nothing came out. Ha ha! Dry as a bone, completely wasted, this pretty little thing God gave me between my legs. Well I am going to have lovers now, you fucks! Like in the movies, big shoulders and all, and a summer house, and nice trips, and in the morning in my room a big vase of flowers, and I'm going to get my nipples hard standing in the breeze from the ocean, eating shrimp from a cup, you sons of bitches, while my lover watches me from the veranda, his big shoulders shining, all hard for me, that's one damn thing I will guarantee you kids! Ha ha! You think I'm joking? I ain't freaking joking. I never got nothing! My life was shit! I was never even up in a freaking plane. But that was that life and this is this life. My new life. Cover me up now! With a blanket. I need my beauty rest. Tell anyone I'm here, you all die. Plus they die. Whoever you tell, they die. I kill them with my mind. I can do that. I am very freaking strong now. I got powers! So no visitors. I don't exactly look my best. You got it? You all got it?"

We nod. I go for a blanket. Her hands and feet are shaking and she's grinding her teeth and one falls out.

"Put it over me, you fuck, all the way over!" she screams, and I put it over her.

We sneak off with the babies and whisper in the kitchen.

"It looks like her," says Min.

"It is her," I say.

"It is and it ain't," says Jade.

"We better do what she says," Min says.

"No shit," Jade says.

All night she sits in the rocker under the blanket, shaking and swearing.

All night we sit in Min's bed, fully dressed, holding hands.

"See how strong I am!" she shouts around midnight, and there's a cracking sound, and when I go out the door's been torn off the microwave but she's still sitting in the chair.

IN THE MORNING she's still there, shaking and swearing.

"Take the blanket off!" she screams. "It's time to get this show on the road."

I take the blanket off. The smell is not good. One ear is now in her lap. She keeps absentmindedly sticking it back on her head.

"You, Jade!" she shouts. "Get dressed. Go get that job. When you meet Len, bend forward a little. Let him see down your top. Give him some hope. He's a sicko, but we need him. You, Min! Make breakfast. Something home-made. Like biscuits."

"Why don't you make it with your powers?" says Min.

"Don't be a smartass!" screams Bernie. "You see what I did to that microwave?"

"I don't know how to make freaking biscuits," Min wails.

"You know how to read, right?" Bernie shouts. "You ever heard of a recipe? You ever been in the grave? It sucks so bad! You regret all the things you never did. You little bitches are gonna have a very bad time in the grave unless you get on the stick, believe me! Turn down the thermo-stat! Make it cold. I like cold. Something's off with my body. I don't feel right."

I turn down the thermostat. She looks at me.

"Go show your cock!" she shouts. "That is the first part of Phase One. After we get the new place, that's the end of the first part of Phase Two. You'll still show your cock, but only three days a week. Because you'll start commu-nity college. Pre-law. Pre-law is best. You'll be a whiz. You ain't dumb. And Jade'll work weekends to make up for the decrease in cock money. See? See how that works? Now get out of here. What are you gonna do?"

"Show my cock?" I say.

"Show your cock, that's right," she says, and brushes back her hair with her hand, and a huge wad comes out, leaving her almost bald on one side.

"Oh God," says Min. "You know what? No way me and the babies are staying here alone."

"You ain't alone," says Bernie. "I'm here."

"Please don't go," Min says to me.

"Oh, stop it," Bernie says, and the door flies open and I feel a sort of invisible fist punching me in the back.

Outside it's sunny. A regular day. A guy's changing his oil. The clouds are regular clouds and the sun's the regular sun and the only nonregular thing is that my clothes smell like Bernie, a combo of wet cellar and rotten bacon.

Work goes well. I manage to keep smiling and hide my shaking hands, and my midshift rating is Honeypie. After lunch this older woman comes up and says I look so much like a real Pilot she can hardly stand it.

On her head is a thumbprint. Like Ash Wednesday, only sort of glowing.

I don't know what to do. Do I just come out and ask if she wants to see my cock? What if she says no? What if I get caught? What if I show her and she doesn't think it's worth twenty bucks?

Then she asks if I'll surprise her best friend with a birthday table dance. She points out her friend. A pretty girl, no thumbprint. Looks somehow familiar.

We start over and at about twenty feet I realize it's Angela.

Angela Silveri.

We dated senior year. Then Dad died and Ma had to take a job at Patty-Melt Depot. From all the grease Ma got a bad rash and could barely wear a blouse. Plus Min was running wild. So Angela would come over and there'd be Min getting high under a tarp on the carport and Ma sitting in her bra on a kitchen stool with a fan pointed at her gut. Angela had dreams. She had plans. In her notebook she pasted a picture of an office from the J. C. Penney catalogue and under it wrote, *My (someday?) office.* Once we saw this black Porsche and she said very nice but make hers red. The last straw was Ed Edwards, a big drunk, one of Dad's cousins. Things got so bad Ma rented him the utility room. One night Angela and I were making out on the couch late when Ed came in soused and started peeing in the dishwasher.

What could I say? He's only barely related to me? He hardly ever does that?

Angela's eyes were like these little pies.

I walked her home, got no kiss, came back, cleaned up the dishwasher as best I could. A few days later I got my class ring in the mail and a copy of *The Prophet.*

You will always be my first love, she'd written inside. *But now my path converges to a higher ground. Be well always. Walk in joy. Please don't think me cruel, it's just that I want so much in terms of accomplishment, plus I couldn't believe that guy peed right on your dishes.*

No way am I table dancing for Angela Silveri. No way am I asking Angela Silveri's friend if she wants to see my cock. No way am I hanging around here so Angela can see me in my flight jacket and T-backs and wonder to herself how I went so wrong etc. etc.

I hide in the kitchen until my shift is done, then walk home very, very slowly because I'm afraid of what Bernie's going to do to me when I get there.

· ⸰ ·

MIN MEETS ME at the door. She's got flour all over her blouse and it looks like she's been crying.

"I can't take any more of this," she says. "She's like falling apart. I mean shit's falling off her. Plus she made me bake a freaking pie."

On the table is a very lumpy pie. One of Bernie's arms is now disconnected and lying across her lap.

"What are you thinking of!" she shouts. "You didn't show your cock even once? You think it's easy making those thumbprints? You try it, smartass! Do you or do you not know the plan? You gotta get us out of here! And to get us out, you gotta use what you got. And you ain't got much. A nice face. And a decent unit. Not huge, but shaped nice."

"Bernie, God," says Min.

"What, Miss Priss?" shouts Bernie, and slams the severed arm down hard on her lap, and her other ear falls off.

"I'm sorry, but this is too fucking sickening," says Min. "I'm going out."

"What's sickening?" says Bernie. "Are you saying I'm sickening? Well, I think you're sickening. So many wonderful things in life and where's your mind? You think with your lazy ass. Whatever life hands you, you take. You're not going anywhere. You're staying home and studying."

"I'm what?" says Min. "Studying what? I ain't studying. Chick comes into my house and starts ordering me to study? I freaking doubt it."

"You don't know nothing!" Bernie says. "What fun is life when you don't know nothing? You can't find your own town on the map. You can't name a single president. When we go to Rome you won't know nothing about the history. You're going to study the World Book. Do we still have those World Books?"

"Yeah right," says Min. "We're going to Rome."

"We'll go to Rome when he's a lawyer," says Bernie.

"Dream on, chick," says Min. "And we'll go to Mars when I'm a stockbreaker."

"Don't you dare make fun of me!" Bernie shouts, and our only vase goes flying across the room and nearly nails Min in the head.

"She's been like this all day," says Min.

"Like what?" shouts Bernie. "We had a perfectly nice day."

"She made me help her try on my bras," says Min.

"I never had a nice sexy bra," says Bernie.

"And now mine are all ruined," says Min. "They got this sort of goo on them."

"You ungrateful shit!" shouts Bernie. "Do you know what I'm doing for you? I'm saving your boy. And you got the nerve to say I made goo on your bras! Troy's gonna get caught in a crossfire in the courtyard. In September. September eighteenth. He's gonna get thrown off his little trike. With one leg twisted under him and blood pouring out of his ear. It's a freaking prophecy. You know that word? It means prediction. You know that word? You think I'm bullshitting? Well I ain't bullshitting. I got the power. Watch this: All day Jade sat licking labels at a desk by a window.

Her boss bought everybody subs for lunch. She's bringing some home in a green bag."

"That ain't true about Troy, is it?" says Min. "Is it? I don't believe it."

"Turn on the TV!" Bernie shouts. "Give me the changer."

I turn on the TV. I give her the changer. She puts on *Nathan's Body Shop*. Nathan says washboard abs drive the women wild. Then there's a close-up of his washboard abs.

"Oh yes," says Bernie. "Them are for me. I'd like to give those a lick. A lick and a pinch. I'd like to sort of straddle those things."

Just then Jade comes through the door with a big green bag.

"Oh God," says Min.

"Told you so!" says Bernie, and pokes Min in the ribs. "Ha ha! I really got the power!"

"I don't get it," Min says, all desperate. "What happens? Please. What happens to him? You better freaking tell me."

"I already told you," Bernie says. "He'll fly about fifteen feet and live about three minutes."

"Bernie, God," Min says, and starts to cry. "You used to be so nice."

"I'm still so nice," says Bernie, and bites into a sub and takes off the tip of her finger and starts chewing it up.

JUST AFTER DAWN she shouts out my name.

"Take the blanket off," she says. "I ain't feeling so good."

I take the blanket off. She's basically just this pile of parts: both arms in her lap, head on the arms, heel of one foot touching the heel of the other, all of it sort of wrapped up in her dress.

"Get me a washcloth," she says. "Do I got a fever? I feel like I got a fever. Oh, I knew it was too good to be true. But okay. New plan. New plan. I'm changing the first part of Phase One. If you see two thumbprints, that means the lady'll screw you for cash. We're in a fix here. We gotta speed this up. There ain't gonna be nothing left of me. Who's gonna be my lover now?"

The doorbell rings.

"Son of a bitch," Bernie snarls.

It's Father Brian with a box of doughnuts. I step out quick and close the door behind me. He says he's just checking in. Perhaps we'd like to talk? Perhaps we're feeling some residual anger about Bernie's situation? Which would of course be completely understandable. Once when he was a young priest someone broke in and drew a mustache on the Virgin Mary with a permanent marker, and for weeks he was tortured by visions of bending back the finger of the vandal until he or she burst into tears of apology.

"I knew that wasn't appropriate," he says. "I knew that by indulging in that fantasy I was honoring violence. And yet it gave me pleasure. I also thought of catching them in the act and boinking them in the head with a rock. I also thought of jumping up and down on their backs until something in their spinal column cracked. Actually I had about a million ideas. But you know what I did instead? I scrubbed and scrubbed our Holy Mother, and soon she was as good as new. Her statue, I mean. She herself of course is always good as new."

From inside comes the sound of breaking glass. Breaking glass and then something heavy falling, and Jade yelling and Min yelling and the babies crying.

"Oops, I guess?" he says. "I've come at a bad time? Look, all I'm trying to do is urge you, if at all possible, to forgive the perpetrators, as I forgave the perpetrator that drew on my Virgin Mary. The thing lost, after all, is only your aunt's body, and what is essential, I assure you, is elsewhere, being well taken care of."

I nod. I smile. I say thanks for stopping by. I take the doughnuts and go back inside.

The TV's broke and the refrigerator's tipped over and Bernie's parts are strewn across the living room like she's been shot out of a cannon.

"She tried to get up," says Jade.

"I don't know where the hell she thought she was going," says Min.

"Come here," the head says to me, and I squat down. "That's it for me. I'm fucked. As per usual. Always the bridesmaid, never the bride. Although come to think of it I was never even the freaking bridesmaid. Look, show your cock. It's the shortest line between two points. The world ain't giving away nice lives. You got a trust fund? You a genius? Show your cock. It's what you got. And remember: Troy in September. On his trike. One leg twisted. Don't forget. And also. Don't remember me like this. Remember me like how I was that night we all went to

Red Lobster and I had that new perm. Ah Christ. At least buy me a stone."

I rub her shoulder, which is next to her foot.

"We loved you," I say.

"Why do some people get everything and I got nothing?" she says. "Why? Why was that?"

"I don't know," I say.

"Show your cock," she says, and dies again.

We stand there looking down at the pile of parts. Mac crawls toward it and Min moves him back with her foot.

"This is too freaking much," says Jade, and starts crying.

"What do we do now?" says Min.

"Call the cops," Jade says.

"And say what?" says Min.

We think about this awhile.

I get a Hefty bag. I get my winter gloves.

"I ain't watching," says Jade.

"I ain't watching either," says Min, and they take the babies into the bedroom.

I close my eyes and wrap Bernie up in the Hefty bag and twistie-tie the bag shut and lug it out to the trunk of the K-car. I throw in a shovel. I drive up to St. Leo's. I lower the bag into the hole using a bungee cord, then fill the hole back in.

Down in the city are the nice houses and the so-so houses and the lovers making out in dark yards and the babies crying for their moms, and I wonder if, other than Jesus, this has ever happened before. Maybe it happens all the time. Maybe there's angry dead all over, hiding in rooms, covered with blankets, bossing around their scared, embarrassed relatives. Because how would we know?

I for sure don't plan on broadcasting this.

I smooth over the dirt and say a quick prayer: If it was wrong for her to come back, forgive her, she never got beans in this life, plus she was trying to help us.

At the car I think of an additional prayer: But please don't let her come back again.

WHEN I GET HOME the babies are asleep and Jade and Min are watching a phone-sex infomercial, three girls in leather jumpsuits eating bananas in slo-mo while across the screen runs a constant disclaimer: "Not Necessarily the Girls Who Man the Phones! Not Necessarily the Girls Who Man the Phones!"

"Them chicks seem to really be enjoying those bananas," says Min in a thin little voice.

"I like them jumpsuits though," says Jade.

"Yeah them jumpsuits look decent," says Min.

Then they look up at me. I've never seen them so sad and beat and sick.

"It's done," I say.

Then we hug and cry and promise never to forget Bernie the way she really was, and I use some Resolve on the rug and they go do some reading in their World Books.

Next day I go in early. I don't see a single thumbprint. But it doesn't matter. I get with Sonny Vance and he tells me how to do it. First you ask the woman would she like a private tour. Then you show her the fake P-40, the Gallery of Historical Aces, the shower stall where we get oiled up, etc. etc. and then in the hall near the rest room you ask if there's anything else she'd like to see. It's sleazy. It's gross. But when I do it I think of September. September and Troy in the crossfire, his little leg bent under him etc. etc.

Most say no but quite a few say yes.

I've got a place picked out at a complex called Swan's Glen. They've never had a shooting or a knifing and the public school is great and every Saturday they have a nature walk for kids behind the clubhouse.

For every hundred bucks I make, I set aside five for Bernie's stone.

What do you write on something like that? LIFE PASSED HER BY? DIED DISAPPOINTED? CAME BACK TO LIFE BUT FELL APART? All true, but too sad, and no way I'm writing any of those.

BERNIE KOWALSKI, it's going to say: BELOVED AUNT.

Sometimes she comes to me in dreams. She never looks good. Sometimes she's wearing a dirty smock. Once she had on handcuffs. Once she was naked and dirty and this mean cat was clawing its way up her front. But every time it's the same thing.

"Some people get everything and I got nothing," she says. "Why? Why did that happen?"

Every time I say I don't know.

And I don't.

THE BOY ON THE BIKE flew by the chink's house, and the squatty-body's house, and the house where the dead guy had rotted for five days, remembering that the chink had once called him nasty, the squatty-body had once called the cops when he'd hit her cat with a lug nut on a string, the chick in the dead guy's house had once asked if he, Cody, ever brushed his teeth. Someday when he'd completed the invention of his special miniaturizing ray he would shrink their houses and flush them down the shitter while in tiny voices all three begged for some sophisticated mercy, but he would only say, Sophisticated? When were you ever sophisticated to me? And from the toilet bowl they would say, Well, yes, you're right, we were pretty mean, flush us down, we deserve it; but no, at the last minute he would pluck them out and place them in his lunchbox so he could send them on secret missions such as putting hideous boogers of assassination in Lester Finn's thermos if Lester Finn ever again asked him in

Civics why his rear smelled like hot cotton with additional crap cling-ons.

It was a beautiful sunny day and the aerobics class at the Rec had let out and cars were streaming out of the parking lot with sun glinting off their hoods, and he rode along on the sidewalk, racing the cars as they passed.

Here was the low-hanging willow where you had to duck down, here was the place with the tilty sidewalk square that served as a ramp when you jerked hard on the handlebars, which he did, and the crowd went wild, and the announcers in the booth above the willow shook their heads, saying, Wow, he takes that jump like there's no tomorrow while them other racers fret about it like some kind of tiny crying babies!

Were the Dalmeyers home?

Their gray car was still in the driveway.

He would need to make another lap.

Yesterday he had picked up a bright-red goalie pad and all three Dalmeyers had screamed at him, Not that pad Cody you dick, we never use those pads in the driveway because they get scuffed, you rectum, those are only for ice, were you born a rectal shitbrain or did you take special rectal shitbrain lessons, in rectal shitbrain lessons did they teach you how to ruin everybody's things?

Well yes, he had ruined a few Dalmeyer things in his life, he had yes pounded a railroad spike in a good new volleyball, he had yes secretly scraped a ski with a nail, he had yes given the Dalmeyer dog Rudy a cut on its leg with a shovel, but that had been an accident, he'd thrown the shovel at a rosebush and stupid Rudy had walked in front of it.

And the Dalmeyers had snatched away the goalie pad and paraded around the driveway making the nosehole sound, and when he tried to laugh to show he was a good sport he made the nosehole sound for real, and they totally cracked up, and Zane Dalmeyer said why didn't he take his trademark nosehole sound on Broadway so thousands could crap their pants laughing? And Eric Dalmeyer said hey if only he had like fifty different-sized noseholes that each made a different sound then he could play songs. And they laughed so hard at the idea of him playing songs on Broadway on his fifty different-sized noseholes that they fell to the driveway thrashing their idiotic Dalmeyer limbs, even Ginnie, the baby Dalmeyer, and ha ha ha that had been a laugh, that had been so funny he had almost gone around one two three four and smashed their cranial cavities with his off-brand gym shoes, which was another puzzling dilemmoid, because why did he have Arroes when every single Dalmeyer, even Ginnie, had the Nikes with the lights in the heel that lit up?

Fewer cars were coming by now from the Rec. The ones that did were going faster, and he no longer tried to race them.

Well, it would be revenge, sweet revenge, when he stuck the lozenge stolen from wood shop up the Dalmeyers' water hose, and the next time they turned the hose on it exploded, and all the Dalmeyers, even Dad Dalmeyer, stood around in their nice tan pants puzzling over it like them guys on *Nova*. And the Dalmeyers were so stupid they would conclude that it had been a miracle, and would call some guys from a science lab to confirm the miracle, and one of the lab guys would flip the wooden lozenge into the air and say to Dad Dalmeyer, You know what, a very clever Einstein lives in your neighborhood and I suggest that in the future you lock this hose up, because in all probability this guy cannot be stopped. And he, Cody, would give the lab guy a wink, and later, as they were getting into the lab van, the lab guy would say, Look, why not come live with us in the experimental space above our lab and help us discover some amazing compounds with the same science brain that apparently thought up this brilliant lozenge, because, frankly, when we lab guys were your age, no way, this lozenge concept was totally beyond us, we were just playing with baby toys and doing baby math, but you, you're really something scientifically special.

And when the Dalmeyers came for a lab tour with a school group they would approach him with their big confident underwater watches and say wow oh boy had they ever missed the boat in terms of him, sorry, they were so very sorry, what was this beaker for, how did this burner work, was it really true that he had built a whole entire *T. rex* from scratch and energized it by taming the miraculous power of cosmic thunder? And down in the basement the *T. rex* would rear up its ugly head and want to have a Dalmeyer snack, but using his special system of codes, pounding on a heat pipe a different number of times for each alphabet letter, he would tell the *T. rex*, No no no, don't eat a single Dalmeyer, although why not lift Eric

Dalmeyer up just for the fun of it on the tip of your tremendous green snout and give him a lesson in what kind of power those crushing jaws would have if he, Cody, pounded out on the heat pipe Kill Kill Kill.

Pedaling wildly now, he passed into the strange and dangerous zone of three consecutive Monte Vistas, and inside of each lived an old wop in a dago tee, and sometimes in the creepy trees there were menacing gorillas he took potshots at from bike-back, but not today, he was too busy with revenge to think about monkeys, and then he was out, into the light, coasting into a happier zone of forthright and elephantine Bueno Verdes that sat very honestly with the big open eyes that were their second-story windows, and in his mind as he passed he said hello HELLO to the two elephants and they in turn said to him in kind Dumbo voices hey Cody HEY CODY.

THE BLOCK WAS shaped something like South America, and as he took the tight turn that was Cape Horn he looked across The Field to his small yellow house, which was neither Monte Vista nor Bueno Verde, but predated the subdivision and smelled like cat pee and hamburger blood and had recently been christened by Mom's boyfriend Daryl, that dick, The House of FIRPO, FIRPO being the word Daryl used to describe anything he, Cody, did that was bad or dorky. Sometimes Mom and Daryl tried to pretend FIRPO was a lovey-dovey term by tousling his hair when they said it, but other times they gave him a poke or pinch and sometimes when they thought he couldn't hear they whispered very darkly and meanly to each other *FIRP attack in progress* and he would go to his room and make the nosehole sound in his closet, after which they would come in and fine him a quarter for each nosehole sound they thought they had heard him make, which was often many, many more than he had actually really made.

Sometimes at night in his room Mom babied him by stroking his big wide head and saying he didn't have to pay all the quarters he owed for making the nosehole sound, but other times she said if he didn't knock it off and lose a few pounds how was he ever going to get a date in junior high, because who wanted to date a big chubby nosehole snorter, and then he couldn't help it, it made him nervous to think of junior high, and he made the nosehole sound and she said, Very funny I hope you're amusing your own self because you're not amusing my ass one bit.

The Dalmeyer house now came into sight.

The Dalmeyer car was gone.

It was Go Time.

The decisive butt-kicking he was about to give the Dalmeyer hose would constitute the end of FIRPO in the world, and all, including Ma, would have to bow down before him, saying, Wow wow wow, do we ever stand corrected in terms of you, how could someone FIRPO hatch and execute such a daring manly plan?

The crowd was on its feet now, screaming his name, and he passed the chink's house again, here was the driveway down which he must turn to cross the street to the

Dalmeyers', but then oh crap he was going too fast and missed it, and the announcers in the booth above the willow gasped in pleasure at his sudden decisive decision to swerve across the newly sodded lawn of the squatty-body's house. His bike made a trough in the sod and went *humpf* over the curb, and as the white car struck him the boy and the bike flew together in a high comic arc across the street and struck the oak on the opposite side with such violence that the bike wrapped around the tree and the boy flew back into the street.

Arghh arghh Daryl will be pissed and say Cody why are you bleeding like a stuck pig you little shit. There was something red wrong with his Arroes. At Payless when they bought the Arroes, Mom said, If you squirm once more you're gonna be facedown on this carpet with my hand whacking your big fat ass. Daryl will say, I buy you a good bike and what do you do, you ruin it. Ma will come up with a dish towel and start swiping at the blood and Daryl will say, Don't ruin that dish towel, he made his bed let him sleep in it, I'll hose him off in the yard, a little shivering won't kill him, he did the crime let him do the time. Or Mom might throw a fit like the night he slipped and fell in the school play, and Ms. Phillips said, Tell your mother, Cody, how you came to slip and fall during the school play so that everyone in the auditorium was looking at you instead of Julia who was at that time speaking her most important line.

And Mom said: Cody are you deaf?

And Ms. Phillips said: He slipped because when I told him stay out of that mopped spot did he do it? No, he did not, he walked right through it on purpose and then down he went.

Which is exactly what he does at home, Mom said. Sometimes I think he's wired wrong.

And Ms. Phillips said, Well, today, Cody, you learned a valuable lesson, which is if someone tells you don't do something, don't do it, because maybe that someone knows something you don't from having lived a longer time than you.

And Daryl said, Or maybe he liked falling on his butt in front of all his friends.

Now a white-haired stickman with no shirt was bending over him, so skinny, touch touch touching him all over, like looking to see if he was wearing a bulletproof vest, doing some very nervous mouthbreathing, with a silver cross hanging down, and around his nipples were sprigs of white hair.

Oh boy, oh God, said the stickman. Say something, pal, can you talk?

And he tried to talk but nothing came, and tried to move but nothing moved.

Oh God, said the stickman, don't go, pal, please say something, stay here with me now, we'll get through this.

What crazy teeth. What a stickman. The stickman's hands flipped around like nervous old-lady hands in movies where the river is rising and the men are away. What a Holy Roller. What a FIRPO. A Holy Roller FIRPO stickman with hairy nips and plus his breath smelled like coffee.

Listen, God loves you, said the stickman. You're going,

okay, I see you're going, but look, please don't go without knowing you are beautiful and loved. Okay? Do you hear me? You are good, do you know that? God loves you. God loves you. He sent His son to die for you.

Oh the freaking FIRPO, why couldn't he just shut up? If the stickman thought he, Cody, was good, he must be FIRPO because he, Cody, wasn't good, he was FIRPO, Mom had said so and Daryl had said so and even Mr. Dean in Science had told him to stop lying the time he tried to tell about seeing the falling star. The announcers in the booth above the willow began weeping as he sat on Mom's lap and said he was very sorry for having been such a FIRPO son and Mom said, Oh thank you, thank you, Cody, for finally admitting it, that makes it nice, and her smile was so sweet he closed his eyes and felt a certain urge to sort of shake things out and oh Christ dance.

You are beautiful, beautiful, the stickman kept saying, long after the boy had stopped thrashing, God loves you, you are beautiful in His sight.

· *The* ·
BARBER'S UNHAPPINESS

1.

MORNINGS THE BARBER LEFT his stylists inside and sat out front of his shop, drinking coffee and ogling every woman in sight. He ogled old women and pregnant women and women whose photographs were passing on the sides of buses and, this morning, a woman with close-cropped black hair and tear-stained cheeks, who wouldn't be half bad if she'd just make an effort, clean up her face a little and invest in some decent clothes, some white tights and a short skirt maybe, knee boots and a cowboy hat and a cigarillo, say, and he pictured her kneeling on a crude Mexican sofa, in a little mud hut, daring him to take her, and soon they'd screwed their way into some sort of bean-field while some gaucho guys played soft guitars, although actually he'd better put the gaucho guys behind some trees or a rock wall so they wouldn't get all hot and bothered from watching the screwing and swoop down and stab him and have their way with Miss Hacienda as he bled to death, and come to think of it, forget the gauchos altogether, he'd just put some soft guitars on the stereo in the hut and leave the door open, although actually what was a stereo doing in a Mexican hut? Were there outlets? Plus how could he meet her? He could compliment her hair, then ask her out for coffee. He could say that as a hair-care professional, he knew a little about hair, and boy did she ever have great hair, and by the way did she like coffee? Except they always said no. Lately no no no was all he got. Plus he had zero access to a beanfield or mud hut. They could do it in his yard but it wouldn't be the same because Jeepers had basically made of it a museum of poop, plus Ma would call 911 at the first hint of a sexy moan.

Now those, those on that meter maid, those were some serious hooters. Although her face was sort of beat. But if you could take those hooters and slap them on Miss Hacienda, wow, then you'd be talking. Just the meter maid's hooters and some decent clothes and a lip wax and the super sexy voice of the librarian who looked away whenever he ogled her, and you'd have his perfect woman, and wow would they ever be happy together forever, as long as she kept a positive attitude, which come to think of it might be an issue, because why the heck was she crying in public?

Miss Hacienda passed through a gap in a hedge and disappeared into the Episcopal church.

Why was she going into church on a weekday? Maybe she had a problem. Maybe she was knocked up. Maybe if he followed her into the church and told her he knew a little about problems, having been born with no toes, she'd have coffee with him. He was tired of going home to just Ma. Lately she'd been falling asleep with her head on his shoulder while they watched TV. Sometimes he worried that somebody would look in the window and wonder why he'd married such an old lady. Plus sometimes he worried that Ma would wake up and catch him watching the black girl in the silver bikini riding her horse through that tidal pool in slow motion on 1-900-DREMGAL.

He wondered how Miss Hacienda would look in a silver bikini in slow motion. Although if she was knocked up she shouldn't be riding a horse. She should be sitting down, taking it easy. Somebody should be bringing her a cup of tea. She should move in with him and Ma. He wouldn't rub it in that she was knocked up. He'd be loving about it. He'd be a good friend to her and wouldn't even try to screw her, and pretty soon she'd start wondering why not and start really wanting him. He'd be her labor coach and cheerfully change diapers in the wee hours and finally when she'd lost all the weight she'd come to his bed and screw his brains out in gratitude, after which he'd have a meditative smoke by the window and decide to marry her. He nearly got tears in his eyes thinking of how she'd get tears in her eyes as he went down on one knee to pop the question, a nice touch the dolt who'd knocked her up wouldn't have thought of in a million years, the nimrod, and that SOB could drive by as often as he wanted, deeply regretting his foolishness as the baby frolicked in the yard, it was too late, they were a family, and nothing would ever break them up.

But he'd have to remember to stick a towel under the

door while meditatively smoking or Ma would have a cow, because after he smoked she always claimed everything smelled like smoke, and made him wash every piece of clothing in the house. And they'd better screw quietly if they weren't married, because Ma was old-fashioned. It was sort of a pain living with Ma. But Miss Hacienda had better be prepared to tolerate Ma, who was actually pretty good company when she stayed on her meds, and so what if she was nearly eighty and went around the house flossing in her bra? It was her damn house. He'd better never hear Miss Hacienda say a word against Ma, who'd paid his way through barber college, like for example asking why Ma had thick sprays of gray hair growing out of her ears, because that would kill Ma, who was always reminding the gas man she'd been a dish in high school. How would Miss Hacienda like it if after a lifetime of hard work she got wrinkled and forgetful and some knocked-up slut dressed like a Mexican cowgirl moved in and started complaining about her ear hair? Who did Miss Hacienda think she was, the Queen of Sheba? She could go into labor in the damn Episcopal church for all he cared, he'd keep wanking it in the pantry on the little milking stool for the rest of his life before he'd let Ma be hurt, and that was final.

As Miss Hacienda came out of the church she saw a thick-waisted, beak-nosed, middle-aged man rise angrily from a wooden bench and stomp into Mickey's Hairport, slamming the door behind him.

2.

Next morning Ma wanted an omelet. When he said he was running late she said never mind in a tone that made it clear she was going to accidentally/on purpose burn herself again while ostensibly making her own omelet. So he made the omelet. When he asked was it good, she said it was fine, which meant it was bad and he had to make pancakes. So he made pancakes. Then he kissed her cheek and flew out the door, very very late for Driving School.

Driving School was being held in what had been a trendy office park in the Carter years and was now a flat white overgrown stucco bunker with tinted windows and a towable signboard that said: *Dirving School*. Inside was a conference table that filled most of a room that smelled like a conference table sitting in direct sunlight with some spilled burned coffee on it.

"Latecomers will be beaten," said the Driving School instructor.

"Sorry," said the barber.

"Joking!" said the instructor, thrusting a disorderly wad of handouts at the barber, who was trying to get his clip-ons off. "What I was just saying was that, our aim is, we're going to be looking at some things or aspects, in terms of driving? Meaning safety, meaning, is speeding something we do in a vacuum, or could it involve a pedestrian or fatality or a family out for a fun drive, and then here you come, speeding, with the safety or destiny of that family not held firmly in your mind, and what happens next? Who knows?"

"A crash?" said someone.

"An accident?" said someone else.

"Crash or accident both could," said the instructor. "Either one might or may. Because I've seen, in my CPR role, as a paramedic, when many times, and I'm sorry if you find this gross or too much, I've had to sit in our rescue vehicle with a cut-off arm or hand, even of a kid, a really small arm or even limb, just weeping as if I hadn't been thoroughly trained, as I know none of you have, but I have, and why was I holding that small arm or limb and bawling? Because of someone like you yourselves, good people, I know you are, I'm not saying that, but you decided what? What did you decide? Or they. That person who cut off that kid's arm I was carrying that day I was just saying?"

No one knew.

"They decided to speed is what you did," said the instructor sadly, with pity for both the armless child and the otherwise good people who on that fateful day had decided to speed, and now sat before him, lives ruined.

"I didn't hit nobody," said a girl in a T-shirt that said *Buggin'*. "Cop just stopped me."

"But I'm talking the possibility aspect?" the instructor said kindly. "I'm talking what happens if you walk away from here a man or woman not changed in her thought patterns by the material I'm about to present you in terms of the visuals and graphics? Which some of the things are crashes and some are working wounds I myself have personally dressed and some are wounds we downloaded off the Internet so you could have a chance to see wounds that are national? Because why? Because consequences. Because are we on this earth or an island?"

"Oh," said the Buggin' girl, who now seemed chastened and convinced.

Outside the tinted window were a little forest and a stream and an insurance agency and a FedEx drop-off tilted by some pipeline digging. There were six students. One was the barber. One was a country boy with a briefcase, who took laborious notes and kept asking questions with a furrowed brow, as if, having been caught speeding, he was now considering a career in law enforcement. Did radar work via sonar beams? How snotty did someone have to get before you could stun them with your stun gun? Next to the country boy was the Buggin' girl. Next to the Buggin' girl was a very very happy crew-cut older man in a cowboy shirt and bolo tie who laughed at everything and seemed to consider it a great privilege to be here at the Driving School on this particular day with this particular bunch of excellent people, and who by the end of the session had proposed holding a monthly barbecue at his place so they wouldn't lose touch. Across the table from the Happy Man was a white-haired woman about the barber's age, who kept making sly references to films and books the barber had never heard of and rolling her eyes at things the instructor said, while writing *Help Me!* and *Beam Me Up!* on her notepad and shoving it across the table for the Happy Man to read, which seemed to make the Happy Man uncomfortable.

Next to the white-haired woman was a pretty girl. A
very pretty girl. Wow. One of the prettiest girls the barber
had ever seen. Boy was she pretty. Her hair was crimped
and waist-length and her eyes were doelike and Egyptian
and about her there was a sincerity and intelligence that
made it hard for him to look away. She certainly looked
out of place here at the conference table, with one hand
before her in a strip of sunlight that shone on a very pretty
turquoise ring that seemed to confirm her as someone
exotic and darkish and schooled in things Eastern, someone you could easily imagine making love to on a barge
on the Nile, say, surrounded by thousands of candles that
smelled weird, or come to think of it maybe she was
American Indian, and he saw her standing at the door of
a tipi wearing that same sincere and intelligent expression
as he came home from the hunt with a long string of dead
rabbits, having been accepted into the tribe at her request
after killing a cute white rabbit publicly to prove he was a
man of the woods, or actually they had let him skip the
rabbit part because he had spoken to them so frankly about
the white man's deviousness and given them secret information about an important fort after first making them
promise not to kill any women or children. He pictured
one of the braves saying to her, as she rubbed two corncobs together in the dying sunlight near a spectacular mesa,
that she was lucky to have the barber, who had powerful
medicine in terms of being a powerful medicine man, and
silently she smiled, rubbing the corncobs together perhaps
a little faster, remembering the barber naked in their tipi,

although on closer inspection it appeared she was actually probably Italian.

The girl looked up and caught him staring at her. He dropped his eyes and began leafing through his course materials.

After a number of slides of terrible wounds, the instructor asked did anyone know how many g's a person pulled when he or she went through a windshield at eighty miles per after hitting a bridge abutment or cow. No one knew. The instructor said quite a few. The Happy Man said he'd had a feeling it was quite a few, which was why, wasn't it, that people died? The instructor said either that or flying debris or having one's torso absolutely crushed.

"I guess that would do it," said the Happy Man, grinning.

"So what's my point?" the instructor said, pointing with his pointer to an overhead of a cartoon man driving a little car toward a tombstone while talking gaily on a car phone. "Say we're feeling good, very good, or bad, which is the opposite, say we've just had a death or a promotion or the birth of a child or a fight with our wife or spouse, but my point is, we're experiencing an emotional peak? Because what we then maybe forget, whether happy or fighting or sad or glad, whatever, is that two tons of car is what, is the thing you are in, inside of, driving, and I hope not speeding or otherwise, although for the sake of this pretend example I'm afraid we have to assume yes, you are, which is how this next bad graphic occurs."

Now on the overhead the cartoon man's body parts

were scattered and his car phone was flying up to heaven on little angel wings. The barber looked at the pretty girl again. She smiled at him. His heart began to race. This never happened. They never smiled back. Well, she was young. Maybe she didn't know better than to smile back at an older guy you didn't want. Or maybe she wanted him. It was possible. Maybe she'd had it with young horny guys just out for quick rolls in the hay. Maybe she wanted someone old enough to really appreciate her, who didn't come too quickly and owned his own business and knew how to pick up after himself. He hoped she was a very strict religious virgin who'd never even had a roll in the hay. Not that he hoped she was frigid. He hoped she was the kind of strict religious virgin who, once married, would let it all hang out, and when not letting it all hang out would move with quiet dignity in conservative clothes so that no one would suspect how completely and totally she could let it all hang out when she chose to, and that she came from a poor family and could therefore really appreciate the hard work that went into running a small business, and maybe even had some accounting experi- ence and could help with the books. Although truth- fully, even if she'd had hundreds of rolls in the hay and couldn't add a stinking row of figures, he didn't care, she was so pretty, they'd work it out, assuming of course she'd have him, and with a sinking heart he remembered his missing toes. He remembered that day at the lake with Mary Ellen Kovski, when it had been over a hundred and he'd sat on a beach chair fully dressed, claiming to be chilly. A crowd of Mary Ellen's friends had gathered to help her undress him and throw him in, and in desperation he'd whispered to her about his toes, and she'd gone white and called off her friends and two months later married Phil Anpesto, that idiotic beanpole. Oh, he was tired of hiding his toes. He wanted to be open about them. He wanted to be loved in spite of them. Maybe this girl had a wisdom beyond her years. Maybe her father had a deformity, a glass eye or facial scar, maybe through long years of loving this kindly but deformed man she had come to almost need the man she loved to be somewhat deformed. Not that he liked the idea of her trotting after a bunch of deformed guys, and also not that he considered himself deformed, exactly, although, admittedly, ten barely discernible bright-pink nubs were no picnic. He pictured her lying nude in front of a fireplace, so comfortable with his feet that she'd given each nub a pet name, and maybe sometimes during lovemaking she got a little carried away and tried to kiss or lick his nubs, although certainly he didn't expect that, and in fact found it sort of disgusting, and for a split second thought somewhat less of her, then pictured himself gently pulling her up, away from his feet, and the slightly shamed look on her face made him forgive her completely for the disgusting thing she'd been about to do out of her deep deep love for him.

The instructor held up a small bloodied baby doll, which he then tossed across the room into a trunk.

"Blammo," he said. "Let's let that trunk represent a crypt or tomb, and it's your fault, from speeding, how then do you feel?"

"Bad," said the Buggin' girl.

The pretty girl passed the barber the Attendance Log, which had to be signed to obtain Course Credit and Associated Conviction Waivers / Point Reductions.

They looked frankly at each other for what felt like a very long time.

"Hokay!" the instructor said brightly. "I suppose I don't have to grind you into absolute putty, so now it's a break, so you don't view me as some sort of Marquis de Sade or harsh taskmaster requiring you to watch gross visuals and graphics until your mind rots out."

The barber took a deep breath. He would speak to her. Maybe buy her a soda. The girl stood up. The barber got a shock. Her face was the same lovely exotic intelligent slim Cleopatran face, but her body seemed scaled to a head twice the size of the one she had. She was a big girl. Her arms were round and thick. Her mannerisms were a big girl's mannerisms. She hunched her shoulders and tugged at her smock. He felt a little miffed at her for having misled him and a little miffed at himself for having ogled such a fatty. Well, not a fatty, exactly, her body was okay, it seemed solid enough, it was just too big for her head. If you could somehow reduce the body to put it in scale with the head, or enlarge the head and shrink down the entire package, then you'd have a body that would do justice to that beautiful beautiful face that, even now, tidying up his handouts, he was regretting having lost.

"Hi," she said.

"Hello," he said, and went outside and sat in his car, and when she came out with two Cokes pretended to be cleaning the ashtrays until she went away.

3.

Later that month the barber sat stiffly at a wedding recep-
tion at the edge of a kind of mock Japanese tearoom at
the Hilton while some goofball inside a full-body
PuppetPlayers groom costume, complete with top hat and
tails and a huge yellow felt head and three-fingered yellow
felt hands, made vulgar thrusting motions with his hips in
the barber's direction, as if to say: Do you like to do this?
Have you done this? Can you show me how to do this,
because soon I'm going to have to do this with that
PuppetPlayers bride over there who is right now flirting—
hey!—flirting with that bass player! and the PuppetPlayers
groom sprinted across the dance floor and began romp-
ing pugilistically around the bass player who'd been trying
to cuckold him. Everyone was laughing and giving the barber inexplicable thumbs-ups as the PuppetPlayers groom
dragged the PuppetPlayers bride across the dance floor
and introduced her to the barber, and she appeared to be
very taken with him, and sat on his lap and forced his
head into her yellow felt cleavage, which was stained
with wine and had a cigarette burn at the neckline. With
many gestures she bade the barber look under her skirts,
and overcome with embarrassment he did so, eventually
finding a wrapped box which, when opened, revealed a
wrapped cylinder which, when opened, shot a banner
across the dance floor, and on the banner was written:
BEST O' LUCK ARNIE & EVELYN FROM MOM AND POP.

The PuppetPlayers newlyweds sprinted across the room and bowed low before Arnie and Evelyn, who were sitting sullenly on the bandstand, apparently in the middle of a snit.

"Mickey!" Uncle Edgar shouted to the barber. "Mickey, you should've boffed that puppet broad! So what if she's a puppet! You're no prize! You're going to be choosy? Think of it! Think of it! Arnie's half your age!"

"Edgar for Christ's sake you're embarrassing him!" shouted Aunt Jean. "It's like you're saying he's old! It's like you're saying he's an old maid, only he's a guy! See what I mean? You think that's nice?"

"I am!" shouted Uncle Edgar, "I am saying that! He's a damned old lady! I don't mean no offense! I'm just saying get out and live! I love him! That's why I'm saying! The sun's setting! Pork some young babe, and if you like it, if you like the way she porks, what the hell, put down roots! What do you care? Love you can learn! But you gotta start somewhere! I mean my God, even these little so-and-sos here are trying to get some of it!"

And Uncle Edgar threw a dinner roll at a group of four adolescent boys the barber vaguely remembered having once pulled around the block in a little red wagon. The boys gave Uncle Edgar the finger and confirmed that not only were they trying to get some of it, they were actually getting some of it, and not always from the same chick, and sometimes more than once a day, and sometimes right after football practice, and quite possibly in the near future from a very hot Shop teacher they had reason to believe would probably give it to all of them at once if only they approached it the right way.

"Holy cow!" shouted Uncle Edgar. "Let me go to that school!"

"Edgar, you pig, be logical!" shouted Aunt Jean. "Just because Mickey's not married don't mean he ain't getting any! He could be getting some from a lady friend, or several lady friends, lady friends his own age, who already know the score, whose kids are full-grown! You don't know what goes on in his bed at night!"

"At least I don't think he's queer!" Uncle Edgar shouted to the adolescents the barber now remembered having loaded sleeping into a minivan on the evening of the day, years before, when he'd pulled them in the red wagon.

"If he is we don't give a rat's ass," said one of the adolescents. "That's his business."

"We learned that in school," said another. "Who You Do Is Up to You. We had a mini-session."

Now the PuppetPlayers groom was trying to remove the real bride's garter, and some little suited boys were walking a ledge along a goldfish stream that separated the Wedding Area from Okinawa Memories, where several clearly non-Japanese women in kimonos hustled drinks, sounding a huge metal gong whenever anyone ordered a double, at which time a bartender dressed like a sumo sent a plastic sparrow across the room on a guy wire. The little suited boys began prying up the screen that kept the goldfish from going over a tiny waterfall, to see if they would die in a shallow pond near the Vending Area.

"For example those kids torturing those fish," shouted Uncle Edgar. "You know who those kids are? Them are

Brendan's kids. You know who Brendan is? He's Dick's kid. You remember who Dick is? Your second cousin the same age as you, man! Remember I took you guys to the ball-game and he threw up in my Rambler? So them kids are Dick's grandkids and here Dick's the same age as you, which means you're old enough to be a grandpa, grandpa, but you ain't even a pa yet, which I don't know how you feel about it but I think is sort of sad or weird!"

"You do but maybe he don't!" shouted Aunt Jean. "Why do you think everything you think is everything everybody else thinks? Plus Dick's no saint and neither are those kids! Dick was a teen dad and Brendan was a teen dad and probably those kids on that ledge are going to be teen dads as soon as they finish killing those poor fish!"

"Agreed!" shouted Uncle Edgar. "Hey, I got no abiding love for Dick! You want to have a fight with me at a wedding over my feelings for Dick, who throwing up in my Rambler was just the start of the crap he's pulled on me? All's I'm saying is, there's no danger of Mickey here being a teen dad, and he better think about what I'm saying and get on the stick before his shooter ain't a viable shooter anymore!"

"I'm sure you start talking about the poor guy's shooter at a wedding!" shouted Aunt Jean. "You're drunk!"

"Who ain't?" shouted Uncle Edgar, and the table exploded in laughter and one of the adolescents fell mock-drunk off his chair and when this got a laugh all the other adolescents fell mock-drunk off their chairs.

The barber excused himself and walked quickly out of the Wedding Area past three stunning girls in low-cut white gowns, who stood in what would have been shade from the fake overhanging Japanese cherry trees had the trees been outside and had it been daytime.

In the bathroom the Oriental theme receded and all was shiny chrome. The barber peed, mentally defending himself against Uncle Edgar. First off, he'd had plenty of women. Five. Five wasn't bad. Five was more than most guys, and for sure it was more than Uncle Edgar, who'd married Jean right out of high school and had a lower lip like a fish. Who would Uncle Edgar have had him marry? Sara DelBianco, with her little red face? Ellen Wiest, that tall drink of water? Ann DeMann, who was swaybacked and had claimed he was a bad screw? Why in the world was he, a successful small businessman, expected to take advice from someone who'd spent the best years of his life transferring partial flanges from one conveyor belt to another while spraying them with a protective solvent mist? Uncle Edgar could take a flying leap, that drunk, why didn't he mind his own beeswax and spray himself with a protective solvent mist and leave the ambitious entrepreneurs of the world alone, the lush?

The barber wet his comb the way he'd been wetting his comb since high school and prepared to slick back his hair. A big vital man with a sweaty face came in and whacked the barber on the back as if they were old pals. In the mirror was a skeletal mask of blue and purple and pink that the barber knew was his face but couldn't quite believe was his face, because in the past his face had always risen to the occasion. In the past his face could always be counted on to amount to more than the sum of its parts when he smiled winningly, but now when he smiled winningly he looked like a corpse trying to appear cheerful in a wind tunnel. His eyes bulged, his lips were thin, his forehead wrinkles were deep as sticklines in mud. It had to be the lighting. He was ugly. He was old. How had this happened? Who would want him now?

"You look like hell," thundered the big man from a stall, and the barber fled the mirror without slicking back his hair.

As he rushed past the stunning girls, a boy in a fraternity sweatshirt came over. Seeing the barber, he made a comic geriatric coughing noise in his throat, and one of the girls giggled and adjusted her shoulder strap as if to keep the barber from seeing down her dress.

4.

A few weeks before the wedding, the barber had received in the mail a greeting card showing a cowboy roping a steer. The barber's name was scrawled across the steer's torso, and *Me (Mr. Jenks)* across the cowboy.

Here's hoping you will remember me from our driving school, said a note inside, *and attend a small barbecue at my home. My hope being to renew those acquaintances we started back then, which I found enjoyable and which since the loss of my wife I've had far too few of. Please come and bring nothing. As you can see from the cover, I am roping you in, not to brand you, but only to show you my hospitality, I hope. Your friend, Larry Jenks.*

Who was Jenks? Was Jenks the Happy Man? The barber threw the card in the bathroom trash, imagining the Driving School kooks seated glumly on folding chairs in a trailer house. For a week or so the card sat there, cowboy-side up, vaguely reproaching him. Then he took out the trash.

A few days after the wedding he received a second card from Jenks, with a black flower on the front.

A good time was had by all, it said. *Sorry you were unable to attend. Even the younger folks, I think, enjoyed. Many folks took home quite a few sodas, because as I am alone now, I never could have drank that many sodas in my life. This note, on a sadder note, and that is why the black flower, is to inform you that Eldora Ronsen is moving to Seattle. You may remember her as the older woman to your immediate right. She is high up in her company and just got higher, which is good for her, but bad for us, as she is such a super gal. Please join us Tuesday next, Corrigan's Pub, for farewell drinks, map enclosed, your friend, Larry Jenks.*

Tuesday next was tomorrow.

"Well, you can't go," Ma said. "The girls are coming over."

The girls were the Altar and Rosary Society. When they came over he had to wait on them hand and foot while they talked about which priest they would marry if only the priests weren't priests. When one lifted her blouse to show her recent scar, he had to say it was the worst scar ever. When one asked if her eye looked rheumy he had to get very close to her rheumy eye and say it looked non-rheumy to him.

"Well, I think I might want to go," he said.

"I just said you can't," she said. "The girls are coming."

She was trying to guilt him. She was always trying to guilt him. Once she'd faked a seizure when he tried to go to Detroit for a hair show. No wonder he had no friends. Not that he had no friends. He had plenty of friends. He had Rick the mailman. Every day when Rick the mailman came in, he asked the barber how it was hanging, and the barber said it was hanging fine. He had old Mr. Mellon, at Mellon Drugs, next door to the shop, who, though sort of deaf, was still a good friend, when not hacking phlegm into his little red cup.

"Ma," he said. "I'm going."

"Mr. Bigshot," she said. "Bullying an old lady."

"I'm not bullying you," he said. "And you're not old."

"Oh, I'm young, I'm a tiny baby," she said, tapping her dentures.

That night he dreamed of the pretty but heavy girl. In his dream she was all slimmed down. Her body looked like the body of Daisy Mae in the Li'l Abner cartoon, who he had always found somewhat attractive. She came into the shop in cut-off jeans, chewing a blade of grass, and said she found his accomplishments amazing, especially considering the hardships he'd had to overcome, like his dad dying young and his mother being so nervous, and then she took the blade of grass out of her mouth and put it on the magazine table and stretched out across the Waiting Area couch while he undressed, and seeing his unit she said it was the biggest unit she'd ever seen, and arched her back in a sexy way, and then she called him over and gave him a deep warm kiss on the mouth that was so much like the kiss he'd been waiting for all his life that it abruptly woke him.

Sitting up in bed, he missed her. He missed how much she loved and understood him. She knew everything about him and yet still liked him. His gut sort of ached with wanting.

In his boyhood mirror he caught sight of himself and flexed his chest the way he used to flex his chest in the weightlifting days, and looked so much like a little old man trying to take a dump in his bed that he hopped up and stood panting on the round green rug.

Ma was blundering around in the hallway. Because of the dream he had a partial bone. To hide his partial bone, he kept his groin behind the door as he thrust his head into the hall.

"I was walking in my sleep," Ma said. "I'm so worried I was walking in my sleep."

"What are you worried about?" he said.

"I'm worried about when the girls come," she said.

"Well, don't worry," he said. "It'll be fine."

"Thanks a million," she said, going back into her room. "Very reassuring."

Well, it would be fine. If they ran out of coffee, one of the old ladies could make coffee, if they ran out of snacks they could go a little hungry, if something really disastrous happened they could call him at Corrigan's, he'd leave Ma the number.

Because he was going.

In the morning he called Jenks and accepted the invitation, while Ma winced and clutched her stomach and pulled over a heavy wooden chair and collapsed into it.

5.

Corrigan's was meant to feel like a pub at the edge of a Scottish golf course, there was a roaring fire, and many ancient-looking golf clubs hanging above tremendous tables of a hard plastic material meant to appear gnarled and scarred, and kilted waitresses with names like Heather and Zoe were sloshing chicken wings and fried cheese and lobster chunks into metal vats near an aerial photo of the Old Course at St. Andrews, Scotland.

The barber was early. He liked to be early. He felt it was polite to be early, except when he was late, at which time he felt being early was anal. Where the heck was everybody? They weren't very polite. He looked down at his special shoes. They were blocky and black and had big removable metal stays in the sides and squeaked when he walked. Well if anybody said anything about his shoes they could go to hell, he hadn't asked to be born with no toes, and besides, the special shoes looked nice with khakis.

"Sorry we're late!" Mr. Jenks shouted, and the Driving School group settled in around the long gnarled table.

The pretty but heavy girl hung her purse across the back of her chair. Her hair looked like her hair in the dream and her eyes looked like her eyes in the dream, and as for her body, he couldn't tell, she was wearing a mumu. But certainly facially she was pretty. Facially she was very possibly the prettiest girl here. Was she? If aliens came down and forced each man to pick one woman to reproduce with in a chain-link enclosure while they took notes, would he choose her, based solely on face? Here was a woman with a good rear but a doglike face, here was a woman with a nice perm but a blop at the end of her nose, here was the Buggin' girl, who looked like a chicken, here was the white-haired woman, whose face was all wrinkled, here was the pretty but heavy girl. Was she the prettiest? Facially? He thought she very possibly was.

He regarded her fondly from across the table, waiting for her to catch him regarding her fondly, so he could quickly avert his eyes, so she'd know he was still possibly interested, and then she dropped her menu and bent to retrieve it and the barber had a chance to look briefly down her dress.

Well she definitely had something going on in the chest category. So facially she was the prettiest in the room, plus she had decent boobs. Attractive breasts. The thing was, would she want him? He was old. Oldish. When he stood up too fast his knee joints popped. Lately his gums had started to bleed. Plus he had no toes. Although why sell himself short? He owned his own small business. He had a bit of a gut, yes, and his hair was somewhat thin, but then again his shoulders and chest were broad, so that the over-all effect, even with the gut, was of power, which girls liked, and at least his head was properly sized for his body, which was more than she could say, although then again he still lived with his mother.

Well, who was perfect? He wasn't perfect and she wasn't perfect but they obviously had some sort of special chemistry, based on what had happened at the Driving

School, and anyway, what the heck, he wasn't proposing, he was just considering possibly trying to get to know her somewhat better.

In this way he decided to ask the pretty but heavy girl out.

How to do it, that was the thing. How to ask her. He could get her alone and say her hair looked super. While saying it looked super he could run a curl through his fingers in a professional way, as if looking for split ends. He could say he'd love a chance to cut such excellent hair, then slip her a card for One Free Cut and Coffee. That could work. That had worked in the past. It had worked with Sylvia Reynolds, a bank teller with crow's-feet and a weird laugh who turned out to be an excellent kisser. When she'd come in for her Free Cut and Coffee, he'd claimed they were out of coffee, and taken her to Bean Men Roasters. A few dates later they'd gotten carried away, unfortunately, because of her excellent kissing, and done more, much more actually, than he ever would've imagined doing with someone with crow's-feet and a weird laugh and strangely wide hips, and when he'd gotten home that night and had a good hard look at the locket she'd given him after they'd done it, he'd instantly felt bad, because wow could you ever see the crow's-feet in that picture. As he looked at Sylvia standing in that bright sunlit meadow in the picture, her head thrown back, joyfully laughing, her crow's-feet so very pronounced, a spontaneous image had sprung into his mind of her coming wide-hipped toward him while holding a baby, and suddenly he'd been deeply disappointed in himself for doing it with someone so unusual-looking, and to ensure that he didn't make matters worse by inadvertently doing it with her a second time, he'd sort of never called her again, and had even switched banks.

He glanced at the pretty but heavy girl and found her making her way toward the Ladies'.

Now was as good a time as any.

He waited a few minutes, then excused himself and stood outside the Ladies' reading ads posted on a corkboard until the pretty but heavy girl came out.

He cleared his throat and asked was she having fun? She said yes.

Then he said wow did her hair look great. And in terms of great hair, he knew what he was talking about, he was a professional. Where did she have it cut? He ran one of her curls through his fingers, as if looking for split ends, and said he'd love the chance to work with such dynamite hair, and took from his shirt pocket the card for One Free Cut and Coffee.

"Maybe you could stop by sometime," he said.

"That's nice of you," she said, and blushed.

So she was a shy girl. Sort of cutely nerdy. Not exactly confident. That was too bad. He liked confidence. He found it sexy. On the other hand, who could blame her, he could sometimes be very intimidating. Also her lack of confidence indicated he could perhaps afford to be a little bit bold.

"Like, say, tomorrow?" he said. "Like, say, tomorrow at noon?"

"Ha," she said. "You move quick."

"Not too quick, I hope," he said.

"No," she said. "Not too quick."

So he had her. By saying he wasn't moving too quick, wasn't she implicitly implying that he was moving at exactly the right speed? All he had to do now was close the deal.

"I'll be honest," he said. "I've been thinking about you since Driving School."

"You have?" she said.

"I have," he said.

"So you're saying tomorrow?" she said, blushing again.

"If that's okay for you," he said.

"It's okay for me," she said.

Then she started uncertainly back to the table and the barber raced into the Men's. Yes! Yes yes yes. It was a date. He had her. He couldn't believe it. He'd really played that smart. What had he been worried about? He was cute, women had always considered him cute, never mind the thin hair and minor gut, there was just something about him women liked.

Wow she was pretty, he had done very very well for himself.

Back at the table Mr. Jenks was taking Polaroids. He announced his intention of taking six shots of the Driving School group, one for each member to keep, and the barber stood behind the pretty but heavy girl, with his hands on her shoulders, and she reached up and gave his wrist a little squeeze.

6.

At home old-lady cars were in the driveway and old-lady coats were piled on the couch and the house smelled like old lady and the members of the Altar and Rosary Society were gathered around the dining room table looking frail. They all looked the same to the barber, he could never keep them straight, there was a crone in a lime pantsuit and a crone in a pink pantsuit and two crones in blue pantsuits. As he came in they began asking Ma where he had been, why was he out so late, why hadn't he been here to help, wasn't he normally a fairly good son? And Ma said yes, he was normally a fairly good son, except he hadn't given her any grandkids yet and often wasted water by bathing twice a day.

"My son had that problem," said one of the blue crones. "His wife once pulled me aside."

"Has his wife ever pulled you aside?" the pink crone said to Ma.

"He's not married," said Ma.

"Maybe the not-married is related to the bathing-too-often," said the lime crone.

"Maybe he holds himself aloof from others," said the blue crone. "My son held himself aloof from others."

"My daughter holds herself aloof from others," said the pink crone.

"Does she bathe too often?" said Ma.

"She doesn't bathe too often," said the pink crone. "She just thinks she's smarter than everyone."

"Do you think you're smarter than everyone?" asked the lime crone severely, and thank God at that moment Ma reached up and pulled him down by the shirt and roughly kissed his cheek.

"Have a good time?" she said, and the group photo fell out of his pocket and into the dip.

"Very nice," he said.

"Who are these people?" she said, wiping a bit of dip off the photo with her finger. "Are these the people you went to meet? Who is this you're embracing? This big one."

"I'm not embracing her, Ma," he said. "I'm just standing behind her. She's a friend."

"She's big," Ma said. "You smell like beer."

"Did you girls see Mrs. Link last Sunday?" said the lime crone. "Mrs. Link should never wear slacks. When she wears slacks her hips look wide. Her hips are all you see."

"They almost seem to precede her into the church," said the pink crone.

"It's as if she is being accompanied by her own hips," said the lime crone.

"Some men like them big," said one of the blue crones.

"Look at his face," said the other blue crone. "He likes them big."

"The cat who ate the canary," said the lime crone.

"Actually I don't consider her big," said the barber, in

a tone of disinterested interest, looking down over the pink crone's shoulder at the photo.

"Whatever you say," said the lime crone.

"He's been drinking," said Ma.

Oh he didn't care what they thought, he was happy. He jokingly snatched the photo away and dashed up to his room, taking two stairs at a time. These poor old farts, they were all superlonely, which was why they were so damn mean.

Gabby Gabby Gabby, her name was Gabby, short for Gabrielle.

Tomorrow they had a date for lunch.

Breakfast, rather. They'd moved it up to breakfast. While they'd been kissing against her car she'd said she wasn't sure she could wait until lunch to see him again. He felt the same way. Even breakfast seemed a long time to wait. He wished she was sitting next to him on the bed right now, holding his hand, listening through the tiny vined window to the sounds of the crones cackling as they left. In his mind he stroked her hair and said he was glad he'd finally found her, and she said she was glad to have been found, she'd never dreamed that someone so distinguished, with such a broad chest and wide shoulders, could love a girl like her. Was she happy? he tenderly asked. Oh she was so happy, she said, so happy to be sitting next to this accomplished, distinguished man in this amazing house, which in his mind was not the current house, a pea-green ranch with a tilted cracked sidewalk, but a mansion, on a lake, with a smaller house nearby for Ma, down a very

very long wooded path, and he'd paid cash for the mansion with money he'd made from his international chain of barbershops, each of which was an exact copy of his current barbershop, and when he and Gabby visited his London England shop, leaving Ma behind in the little house, his English barbers would always burst into applause and say Jolly Good Jolly Good as the happy couple walked in the door.

"I'm leaving you the dishes, Romeo," Ma shouted from the bottom of the stairs.

7.

Early next morning he sat in the bath, getting ready for his date. Here was his floating wienie, like some kind of sea creature, here were his nubs on the green tile. He danced them nervously around a bit, like Fred Astaire dancing on a wall, and swirled the washrag through the water, holding it by one corner, so that it too was like a sea creature, a blue ray, a blue monogrammed ray that now crossed the land that was his belly and attacked the sea creature that was his wienie, and remembering what Uncle Edgar had said at the wedding about his shooter not being viable, he gave his shooter a good, hard, reassuring shake, as if congratulating it for being so very viable. It was a great shooter, very good, perfectly fine, in spite of what Ann DeMann had once said about him being a bad screw, it had gotten hard quick last night and stayed hard throughout the kissing, and as far as being queer, that was laughable, he wished Uncle Edgar could have seen that big boner.

Oh he felt good, in spite of a slight hangover he was very happy.

Flipping his unit carelessly from side to side with thumb and forefinger, he looked at the group Polaroid, which he'd placed near the sink. God, she was pretty. He was so lucky. He had a date with a pretty young girl. Those crones were nuts, she wasn't big, no bigger than any other girl. Not much bigger anyway. How wide were her shoulders compared to, say, the shoulders of the Buggin' girl? Well, he wasn't going to dignify that with a response. She was perfect just the way she was. He leaned out of the tub to look closer at the photo. Well, Gabby's shoulders were maybe a little wider than the Buggin' girl's shoulders. Definitely wider. Were they wider than the shoulders of the white-haired woman? Actually in the photo they were even wider than the shoulders of the country boy.

Oh, he didn't care, he just really liked her. He liked her laugh and the way she had of raising one eyebrow when skeptical, he liked the way that, when he moved his hand to her boob as they leaned against her car, she let out a happy little sigh. He liked how, after a few minutes of kissing her while feeling her boobs, which were super, very firm, when he dropped his hand down between her legs, she said she thought that was probably enough for one night, which was good, it showed good morals, it showed she knew when to call it quits.

Ma was in her room, banging things around.

Because for a while there he'd been worried. Worried she wasn't going to stop him. Which would have been disappointing. Because she barely knew him. He could've been anybody. For a few minutes there against the car he'd wondered if she wasn't a little on the easy side. He wondered this now. Did he? Did he wonder this now? Did he want to wonder this now? Wasn't that sort of doubting her? Wasn't that sort of disloyal? No, no, it was fine, there was no sin in looking at things honestly. So was she? Too easy? In other words, why so sort of desperate? Why had she so quickly agreed to go out with him? Why so willing to give it away so easily to some old guy she barely knew? Well, he thought he might know why. Possibly it was due to her size. Possibly the guys her own age had passed her by, due to the big bod, and nearing thirty, she'd heard her biologic clock ticking and decided it was time to lower her standards, which, possibly, was where he came in. Possibly, seeing him at the Driving School, she'd thought: Since all old guys like young girls, big bods notwithstanding, this old pear-shaped balding guy can ergo be had no problem.

Was that it? Was that how it was?

"Some girl just called," Ma said, leaning heavily against the bathroom door. "Some girl, Gabby or Tabby or something? Said you had a date. Wanted you to know she's running late. Is that the same girl? The same fat girl you were embracing?"

Sitting in the tub, he noticed that his penis was gripped nervously in his fist, and let it go, and it fell to one side, as if it had just passed out.

"Do the girl a favor, Mickey," Ma said. "Call it off. She's

too big for you. You'll never stick with her. You never stick
with anyone. You couldn't even stick with Ellen Wiest, for
crying out loud, who was so wonderful, you honestly
think you're going to stick with this Tabby or Zippy or
whatever?"

Of course Ma had to bring up Ellen Wiest. Ma had
loved Ellen, who had a regal face and great manners and
was always kissing up to Ma by saying what a great mother
Ma was. He remembered the time he and Ellen had hiked
up to Butternut Falls and stood getting wet in the mist,
holding hands, smiling sweetly at each other, which had
really been fun, and she'd said she thought she loved him,
which was nice, except wow she was tall. You could only
hold hands with her for so long before your back started
to hurt. He remembered his back sort of hurting in the
mist. Plus they'd had that fight on the way down. Well,
there were a lot of things about Ellen that Ma wasn't aware
of, such as her nasty temper, and he remembered Ellen
storming ahead of him on the trail, glaring back now and
then, just because he'd made a funny remark about her
height, about her blocking out the sun, and hadn't he also
said something about her being able to eat leaves from the
tallest of the trees they were passing under? Well, that had
been funny, it had all been in fun, why did she have to get
so mad about it? Where was Ellen now? Hadn't she married Ed Trott? Well, Trott could have her. Trott was probably suffering the consequences of being married to Miss
Thin Skin even now, and he remembered having recently
seen Ed and Ellen at the ValueWay, Ellen pregnant and
looking so odd, with her big belly pressing against the cart

as she craned that giraffelike neck down to nuzzle Ed, who had a big stupid happy grin on his face like he was the luckiest guy in the world.

The barber stood up angrily from the tub. Here in the mirror were his age-spotted deltoids and his age-spotted roundish pecs and his strange pale love handles.

Ma resettled against the door with a big whump.

"So what's the conclusion, lover boy?" she said. "Are you canceling? Are you calling up and canceling?"

"No I'm not," he said.

"Well, poor her," Ma said.

8.

Every morning of his life he'd walked out between Ma's twin rose trellises. When he went to grade school, when he went to junior high, when he went to high school, when he went to barber college, he'd always walked out between the twin trellises. He walked out between them now, in his brown cords and the blue button-down, and considered plucking a rose for Gabby, although that was pretty corny, he might seem sort of doddering, and instead, using the hand with which he'd been about to pluck the rose, he flicked the rose, then in his mind apologized to the rose for ripping its skin.

Oh, this whole thing made him tense, very tense, he wished he was back in bed.

"Mickey, a word," Ma called out from the door, but he only waved to her over his shoulder.

South Street was an old wagon road. Cars took the bend too fast. Often he scowled at the speeding cars on his way to work, imagining the drivers laughing to themselves about the way he walked. Because on days when his special shoes hurt he sort of minced. They hurt today. He shouldn't have worn the thin gray socks. He was mincing a bit but trying not to, because what if Gabby drove up South on her way to meet him at the shop and saw him mincing?

On Fullerton were three consecutive houses with swing sets. Under each swing was a grassless place. At the last of the three houses a baby sat in the grassless place, smacking a swing with a spoon. He turned up Lincoln Ave, and passed the Liquor Mart, which smelled like liquor, and La Belle Époque, the antique store with the joyful dog inside, and as always the joyful dog sprang over the white settee and threw itself against the glass, and then there was Gabby, down the block, peering into his locked shop, and he corrected his mincing and began walking normally though it killed.

Did she like the shop? He took big bold steps with his head thrown back so he'd look happy. Happy and strong, with all his toes. With all his toes, in the prime of his life. Did she notice how neat the shop was? How professional? Or did she notice that four of the chairs were of one type and the fifth was totally different? Did it seem to her that the shop was geared to old blue-hairs, which was something he'd once heard a young woman say as he took out the trash?

How did she look? Did she look good?

It was still too far to tell.

Now she saw. Now she saw him. Her face brightened, she waved like a little girl. Oh, she was pretty. It was as if he'd known her forever. She looked so hopeful. But oops. Oh my God she was big. She'd dressed all wrong, tight jeans and a tight shirt. As if testing him. Jesus, this was the biggest he'd ever seen her look. What was she doing, testing him by trying to look her worst? Here was an alley, should he swerve into the alley and call her later? Or not? Not call her later? Forget the whole thing? Pretend last night had never happened? Although now she'd seen him. And he didn't want to forget the whole thing. Last night for the first time in a long time he'd felt like someone other than a guy who wanks it on the milking stool in his mother's pantry. Last night he'd bought a pitcher for the Driving School group and Jenks had called him a sport. Last night she'd said he was a sexy kisser.

Thinking about forgetting last night gave him a pit in his stomach. Forgetting last night was not an option. What were the options? Well, she could trim down. That was an option. That was a good option. Maybe all she needed was someone to tell her the simple truth, someone to sit her down and say: Look, you have an incredibly beautiful, intelligent face, but from the neck down, sweetie, wow, we've got some serious work to do. And after their frank talk, she'd send him flowers with a card that said *Thanks for your honesty, let's get this thing done.* And every night as she stood at the mirror in her panties and bra he'd point out places that needed improvement, and the next day she'd energetically address those areas in the gym, and soon the head—bod discrepancy would be eliminated, and he imagined her in a fancy dress at a little table on a veranda, a veranda by the sea, thanking him for the honeymoon trip, she came from a poor family and had never even been on a vacation, much less a six-week tour of Europe, and then she said, Honey why not put down that boring report on how much your international chain of barbershops earned us this month and join me in the bedroom so I can show you how grateful I am, and in the bedroom she started stripping, and was good at it, not that she'd ever done it before, no, she hadn't, she was just naturally good at it, and when she was done, there she was, with her perfect face and the Daisy Mae body, smiling at him with unconditional love.

It wouldn't be easy. It would take hard work. He knew a little about hard work, having made a barbershop out of a former pet store. Tearing out a counter he'd found a dead mouse. From a sump pump he'd pulled three hardened snakes. But he'd never quit. Because he was a worker. He wasn't afraid of hard work. Was she a worker? He didn't know. He'd have to find out.

They'd find out together.

She stood beside his wooden bench, under his shop awning, and the shadow of her dark mane fell at his feet.

What a wild ride this had been, how much he had learned about himself already!

"Here I am," she said, with a shy, pretty smile.

"I'm so glad you are," he said, and bent to unlock the door of the shop.

· THE FALLS ·

MORSE FOUND IT NERVE-WRACKING to cross the St. Jude grounds just as school was being dismissed, because he felt that if he smiled at the uniformed Catholic children they might think he was a wacko or pervert and if he didn't smile they might think he was an old grouch made bitter by the world, which surely, he felt, by certain yardsticks, he was. Sometimes he wasn't entirely sure that he wasn't even a wacko of sorts, although certainly he wasn't a pervert. Of that he was certain. Or relatively certain. Being overly certain, he was relatively sure, was what eventually made one a wacko. So humility was the thing, he thought, arranging his face into what he thought would pass for the expression of a man thinking fondly of his own youth, a face devoid of wackiness or perversion, humility was the thing.

The school sat among maples on a hillside that sloped down to the wide Taganac River, which narrowed and picked up speed and crashed over Bryce Falls a mile downstream near Morse's small rental house, his embarrassingly small rental house, actually, which nevertheless was the best he could do and for which he knew he should be grateful, although at times he wasn't a bit grateful and wondered where he'd gone wrong, although at other times he was quite pleased with the crooked little blue shack covered with peeling lead paint and felt great pity for the poor stiffs renting hazardous shitholes even smaller than his hazardous shithole, which was how he felt now as he came down into the bright sunlight and continued his pleasant walk home along the green river lined with expensive mansions whose owners he deeply resented.

Morse was tall and thin and as gray and sepulchral as a church about to be condemned. His pants were too short, and his face periodically broke into a tense, involuntary grin that quickly receded, as if he had just suffered a sharp pain. At work he was known to punctuate his conversations with brief wild laughs and gusts of inchoate enthusiasm and subsequent embarrassment, expressed by a sudden plunging of the hands into his pockets, after which he would yank his hands out of his pockets, too ashamed of his own shame to stand there merely grimacing for even an instant longer.

From behind him on the path came a series of arrhythmic whacking steps. He glanced back to find Aldo Cummings, an odd duck who, though nearly forty, still lived with his mother. Cummings didn't work and had his bangs cut straight across and wore gym shorts even in the dead of winter. Morse hoped Cummings wouldn't collar him. When Cummings didn't collar him, and in fact passed by without even returning his nervous, self-effacing grin, Morse felt guilty for having suspected Cummings of wanting to collar him, then miffed that Cummings, who collared even the City Hall cleaning staff, hadn't tried to collar him. Had he done something to offend Cummings? It worried him that Cummings might not like him, and it worried him that he was worried about whether a nut like Cummings liked him. Was he some kind of worrywart? It worried him. Why should he be worried, when all he was doing was going home to enjoy his beautiful children without a care in the world, although on the other hand there was Robert's piano recital, which was sure to be a disaster, since Robert never practiced and they had no piano and weren't even sure where or when the recital was and Annie, God bless her, had eaten the cardboard keyboard he'd made for Robert to practice on. When he got home he would make Robert a new cardboard keyboard and beg him to practice. He might even order him to practice. He might even order him to make his own cardboard keyboard, then practice, although this was unlikely, because when he became forceful with Robert, Robert blubbered, and Morse loved Robert so much he couldn't stand to see him blubbering, although if he didn't become forceful with Robert, Robert tended to lie on his bed with his baseball glove over his face.

Good God, but life could be less than easy, not that he was unaware that it could certainly be a lot worse, but to go about in such a state, pulse high, face red, worried sick that someone would notice how nervous one was,

was certainly less than ideal, and he felt sure that his body was secreting all kinds of harmful chemicals and that the more he worried about the harmful chemicals the faster they were pouring out of wherever it was they came from.

When he got home, he would sit on the steps and enjoy a few minutes of centered breathing while reciting his mantra, which was Calm Down Calm Down, before the kids came running out and grabbed his legs and sometimes even bit him quite hard in their excitement and Ruth came out to remind him in an angry tone that he wasn't the only one who'd worked all day, and as he walked he gazed out at the beautiful Taganac in an effort to absorb something of its serenity but instead found himself obsessing about the faulty latch on the gate, which theoretically could allow Annie to toddle out of the yard and into the river, and he pictured himself weeping on the shore, and to eradicate this thought started manically whistling "The Stars and Stripes Forever," while slapping his hands against his sides.

CUMMINGS BOBBED past the restored gristmill, pleased at having so decisively snubbed Morse, a smug member of the power elite in this conspiratorial Village, one of the league of oppressive oppressors who wouldn't know the lot of the struggling artist if the lot of the struggling artist came up with great and beleaguered dignity and bit him on the polyester ass. Over the Pine Street bridge was a fat cloud. To an interviewer in his head, Cummings said he felt the possible rain made the fine bright day even finer and brighter because of the possibility of its loss. The possibility of its ephemeral loss. The ephemeral loss of the day to the fleeting passages of time. Preening time. Preening nascent time, the blackguard. Time made wastrels of us all, did it not, with its gaunt cheeks and its tombly reverberations and its admonishing glances with bony fingers. Bony fingers pointed as if in admonishment, as if to say, "I admonish you to recall your own eventual nascent death, which, being on its way, human, is forthcoming. Forthcoming, mortal coil, and don't think its ghastly pall won't settle on your furrowed brow, *pronto*, once I select your fated number from my very dusty book with this selfsame bony finger with which I'm pointing at you now, you vanity of vanities, you luster, you shirker of duties, as you shuffle after your worldly pleasure centers."

That was some good stuff, if only he could remember it through the rest of his stroll and the coming storm, to scrawl in a passionate hand on his yellow pad. He thought with longing ardor of his blank yellow pad, he thought. He thought with longing ardor of his blank yellow pad, on which, this selfsame day, his fame would be wrought, no — on which, this selfsame day, the first meager scrawlings which would presage his nascent burgeoning fame would be wrought, or rather writ, and someday someone would dig up his yellow pad and virtually cry eureka when they realized what a teeming fragment of minutia, and yet crucial minutia, had been found, and wouldn't all kinds of literary women in short black jackets want to meet him then!

In the future he must always remember to bring his pad everywhere.

THE TOWN HAD SPENT a mint on the riverfront, and now the burbling, smashing Taganac ran past a nail salon in a restored gristmill and a café in a former coal tower and a quaint public square where some high school boys with odd haircuts were trying to kick a soccer ball into the partly open window of a parked Colt with a joy so belligerent and obnoxious that it seemed they believed themselves the first boys ever to walk the face of the earth, which Morse found worrisome. What if Annie grew up and brought one of these freaks home? Not one of these exact freaks, of course, since they were approximately fifteen years her senior, although it was possible that at twenty she could bring home one of these exact freaks, who would then be approximately thirty-five, albeit over Morse's dead body, although in his heart he knew he wouldn't make a stink about it even if she did bring home one of the freaky snots who had just succeeded in kicking the ball into the Colt and were now jumping around joyfully bumping their bare chests together while grunting like walruses, and in fact he knew perfectly well that, rather than expel the thirty-five-year-old freak from his home, he would likely offer him coffee or a soft drink in an attempt to dissuade him from corrupting Annie, who for God's sake was just a baby, because Morse knew very well the kind of man he was at heart, timid of conflict, conciliatory to a fault, pathetically gullible, and with a pang he remembered Len Beck, who senior year had tricked him into painting his ass blue. If there had actually been a secret Blue-Asser's Club, if the ass-painting had in fact been required for membership, it would have been bad enough, but to find out on the eve of one's prom that one had painted one's ass blue simply for the amusement of a clique of unfeeling swimmers who subsequently supplied certain photographs to one's prom date, that was too much, and he had been glad, quite glad actually, at least at first, when Beck, drunk, had tried and failed to swim to Foley's Snag and been swept over the Falls in the dark of night, the great tragedy of their senior year, a tragedy that had mercifully eclipsed Morse's blue ass in the class's collective memory.

Two redheaded girls sailed by in a green canoe, drifting with the current. They yelled something to him, and he waved. Had they yelled something insulting? Certainly it was possible. Certainly today's children had little respect for authority, although one had to admit there was always Ben Akbar, their neighbor, a little Pakistani genius who sometimes made Morse look askance at Robert. Ben was an all-state cellist, on the wrestling team, who was unfailingly sweet to smaller kids and tole-painted and could do a one-handed push-up. Ah, Ben Shmen, Morse thought, ten Bens weren't worth a single Robert, although he couldn't think of one area in which Robert was superior or even equal to Ben, the little smarty-pants, although certainly he had nothing against Ben, Ben being a mere boy, but if Ben thought for a minute that his being more accomplished and friendly and talented than Robert somehow entitled

him to lord it over Robert, Ben had another think coming, not that Ben had ever actually lorded it over Robert.
On the contrary, Robert often lorded it over Ben, or tried
to, although he always failed, because Ben was too sharp to
be taken in by a little con man like Robert, and Morse's
face reddened at the realization that he had just character-
ized his own son as a con man.

Boy oh boy, could life be a torture. Could life ever force
a fellow into a strange, dark place from which he found
himself doing graceless, unforgivable things like casting
aspersions on his beloved firstborn. If only he could escape
BlasCorp and do something significant, such as discover a
critical vaccine. But it was too late, and he had never been
good at biology and in fact had flunked it twice. But some
kind of moment in the sun would certainly not be unwel-
come. If only he could be a tortured prisoner of war who
not only refused to talk but led the other prisoners in rous-
ing hymns at great personal risk. If only he could witness
an actual miracle or save the president from an assassin or
win the Lotto and give it all to charity. If only he could be
part of some great historical event like the codgers he saw
on PBS who had been slugged in the Haymarket Riot or
known Medgar Evers or lost beatific mothers on the
Titanic. His childhood dreams had been so bright, he had
hoped for so much, it couldn't be true that he was a
nobody, although, on the other hand, what kind of somebody spends the best years of his life swearing at a photo-
copier? Not that he was complaining. Not that he was
unaware he had plenty to be thankful for. He loved his
children. He loved the way Ruth looked in bed by candle-

light when he had wedged the laundry basket against the door that wouldn't shut because the house was settling alarmingly, loved the face she made when he entered her, loved the way she made light of the blue-ass story, although he didn't particularly love the way she sometimes trotted it out when they were fighting—for example on the dreadful night when the piano had been repossessed—or the way she blamed their poverty on his passivity within earshot of the kids, or the fact that at the height of her infatuation with Robert's karate instructor, Master Li, she had been dragging Robert to class as often as six times a week, the poor little exhausted guy. But the point was, in spite of certain difficulties, he truly loved Ruth. So what if their bodies were failing and fattening and they undressed in the dark and Robert admired strapping athletes on television while looking askance at Morse's rounded, pimpled back? It didn't matter, because someday, when Robert had a rounded, pimpled back of his own, he would appreciate his father, who had subjugated his petty personal desires for the good of his family, although, God willing, Robert would have a decent career by then and could afford to join a gym and see a dermatologist.

And Morse stopped in his tracks, wondering what in the world two little girls were doing alone in a canoe speeding toward the Falls, apparently oarless.

CUMMINGS WALKED ALONG, gazing into a mythic dusky arboreal Wood that put him in mind of the archetypal vision he had numbered 114 in his "Book of Archetypal Visions," on which Mom that nitwit had recently spilled grape pop. Vision 114 concerned standing on the edge of an ancient dense Wood at twilight, with the safe harbor of one's abode behind and the deep Wild ahead, replete with dark fearsome bears looming from albeit dingy covens. What would that twitching nervous wage-slave Morse think if he were to dip his dim brow into the heady brew that was the "Archetypal Visions"? Morse, ha, Cummings thought, I'm glad I'm not Morse, a dullard in corporate pants trudging home to his threadbare brats in the gathering loam, born, like the rest of his ilk, with their feet of clay thrust down the maw of conventionality, content to cheerfully work lemminglike in moribund cubicles while comparing their stocks and bonds between bouts of tedious lawn-mowing, then chortling while holding their suckling brats to the Nintendo breast. That was a powerful image, Cummings thought, one that he might develop some brooding night into a herculean proem that some Hollywood smoothie would eat like a hotcake, so he could buy Mom a Lexus and go with someone leggy and blowsy to Paris after taking some time to build up his body with arm curls so as to captivate her physically as well as mentally, and in Paris the leggy girl, in perhaps tight leather pants, would sit on an old-time bed with a beautiful shawl or blanket around her shoulders and gaze at him with doe eyes as he stood on the balcony brooding about the Parisian rain and so forth, and wouldn't Morse and his ilk stew in considerable juice when he sent home a postcard just to be nice!

And wouldn't the Village fall before him on repentant

knees when T-shirts imprinted with his hard-won visage, his heraldic leonine visage, one might say, were available to all at the five-and-dime and he held court on the porch in a white Whitmanesque suit while Mom hovered behind him getting everything wrong about his work and proffering inane snacks to his manifold admirers, and wouldn't revenge be sweet when such former football players as Ned Wentz began begging him for lessons in the sonnet? And all that was required for these things to come to pass was some paper and pens and a quixotic blathering talent the likes of which would not be seen again soon, the critics would write, all of which he had in spades, and he rounded the last bend before the Falls, euphoric with his own possibilities, and saw a canoe the color of summer leaves ram the steep upstream wall of the Snag. The girls inside were thrown forward and shrieked with open mouths over frothing waves that would not let them be heard as the boat split open along some kind of seam and began taking on water in doomful fast quantities. Cummings stood stunned, his body electrified, hairs standing up on the back of his craning neck, thinking, I must do something, their faces are bloody, but what, such fast cold water, still I must do something, and he stumbled over the berm uncertainly, looking for help but finding only a farm field of tall dry corn.

MORSE BEGAN TO RUN. In all probability this was silly. In all probability the girls were safe onshore, or if not,

help was already on its way, although certainly it was possible that the girls were not safe onshore and help was not
on its way, and in fact it was even possible that the help that
was on its way was him, which was worrisome, because he
had never been good under pressure and in a crisis often
stood mentally debating possible options with his mouth
hanging open. Come to think of it, it was possible, even
probable, that the boat had already gone over the Falls or
hit the Snag. He remembered the crew of the barge *Fat
Chance,* rescued via rope bridge in the early Reagan years.
He hoped several sweaty, decisive men were already on the
scene and that one of them would send him off to make a
phone call, although what if on the way he forgot the
phone number and had to go back and ask the sweaty,
decisive man to repeat it? And what if this failure got back
to Ruth and she was filled with shame and divorced him
and forbade him to see the kids, who didn't want to see
him anyway because he was such a panicky screw-up? This
was certainly not positive thinking. This was certainly an
example of predestining failure via negativity. Because,
who could tell, maybe he would stand in line assisting the
decisive men and incur a nasty rope burn and go home a
hero wearing a bandage, which might cause Ruth to
regard him in a more favorable sexual light, and they would
stay up all night celebrating his new manhood and
exchanging sweet words between bouts of energetic lovemaking, although what kind of thing was that to be thinking at a time like this, with children's lives at stake? He was
bad, that was for sure. There wasn't an earnest bone in his
body. Other people were simpler and looked at the world

with clearer eyes, but he was self-absorbed and insincere and mucked everything up, and he hoped this wasn't one more thing he was destined to muck up, because mucking up a rescue was altogether different from forgetting to mail out the invitations to your son's birthday party, which he had recently done, although certainly they had spent a small fortune rectifying the situation, stopping just short of putting an actual pony on Visa, but the point was, this was serious, and he had to bear down. And throwing his thin legs out ahead of him, awkwardly bent at the waist, shirt-tails trailing behind and bum knee hurting, he remonstrated with himself to put aside all self-doubt and negativity and prepare to assist the decisive men in whatever way he could once he had rounded the bend and assessed the situation.

But when he rounded the bend and assessed the situation, he found no rope bridge or decisive men, only a canoe coming apart at the base of the Snag and two small girls in matching sweaters trying to bail with a bait bucket. What to do? This was a shocker. Go for help? Sprint to the Outlet Mall and call 911 from Knife World? There was no time. The canoe was sinking before his eyes. The girls would be drowned before he reached Route 8. Could one swim to the Snag? Certainly one could not. No one ever had. Was he a good swimmer? He was mediocre at best. Therefore he would have to run for help. But running was futile. Because there was no time. He had just decided that. And swimming was out of the question. Therefore the girls would die. They were basically dead. Although that couldn't be. That was too sad. What would become of the mother who this morning had dressed them in matching sweaters? How would she cope? Soon her girls would be nude and bruised and dead on a table. It was unthinkable. He thought of Robert nude and bruised and dead on a table. What to do? He fiercely wished himself elsewhere. The girls saw him now and with their hands appeared to be trying to explain that they would be dead soon. My God, did they think he was blind? Did they think he was stupid? Was he their father? Did they think he was Christ? They were dead. They were frantic, calling out to him, but they were dead, as dead as the ancient dead, and he was alive, he was needed at home, it was a no-brainer, no one could possibly blame him for this one, and making a low sound of despair in his throat he kicked off his loafers and threw his long ugly body out across the water.

ABOUT THE AUTHOR

George Saunders is the author of the story collection *Civil-WarLand in Bad Decline*, a finalist for the 1996 PEN/Hemingway Award and a *New York Times* Notable Book for that year. He is also the author of the *New York Times* bestseller *The Very Persistent Gappers of Frip*. His work, which has appeared in *The New Yorker, Harper's,* and *Story,* has received three National Magazine Awards and four times been included in O. Henry Awards collections. He teaches in the Creative Writing Program at Syracuse University.

A NOTE ABOUT THE TYPE

The text of this book is set in Bembo. The display types are Trade Gothic and Bodoni Bold. The book was designed by Judith Stagnitto Abbate, and printed and bound by R. R. Donnelley & Sons in Bloomsburg, Pennsylvania.

Considered one of the most innovative, radical, and brilliant writers working today, George Saunders creates worlds that have cultivated a following of devoted fans. He's a MacArthur "Genius" and a voice for our time and beyond. His work is a movement— startlingly imaginative, sharply observant, and hilarious. Saunders has changed the way we think about storytelling.

"Saunders makes you feel as though you are reading fiction for the first time." **—Khaled Hosseini**

"Few people cut as hard or deep as Saunders does." **—Junot Díaz**

"George Saunders is a complete original. There is no one better, no one more essential to our national sense of self and sanity."
—Dave Eggers

"Not since Twain has America produced a satirist this funny."
—Zadie Smith

"There is no one like him. He is an original—but everyone knows that." **—Lorrie Moore**

"George Saunders makes the all-but-impossible look effortless. We're lucky to have him."
—Jonathan Franzen

"An astoundingly tuned voice—graceful, dark, authentic, and funny—telling just the kinds of stories we need to get us through these times."

—Thomas Pynchon

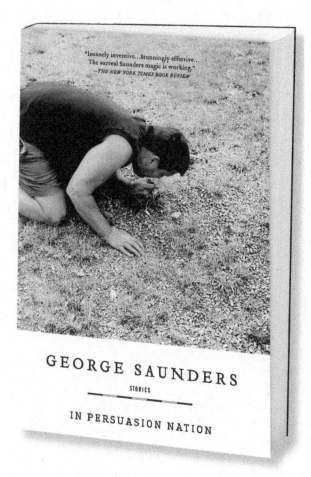

"Insanely inventive...Stunningly effective...
The surreal Saunders magic is working."
—*THE NEW YORK TIMES BOOK REVIEW*

GEORGE SAUNDERS

STORIES

IN PERSUASION NATION

"Insanely inventive . . . Stunningly effective . . . The surreal
Saunders magic is working."

—*The New York Times Book Review*

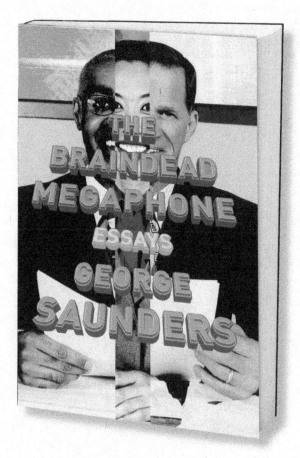

"Saunders's bitingly clever and compassionate essays are a
Mark Twain–style shot in the arm for Americans, an antidote
to the dumbing down virus plaguing our country."

—*Vanity Fair*

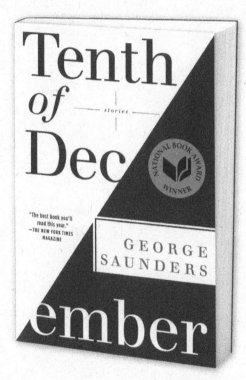

ALSO BY *NEW YORK TIMES*
BESTSELLING AUTHOR

GEORGE SAUNDERS

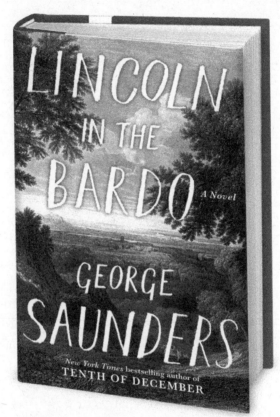

Saunders's long-awaited first novel, about
Abraham Lincoln and the death of his eleven-year-
old son, Willie, at the dawn of the Civil War

A RANDOM HOUSE HARDCOVER AND EBOOK
GeorgeSaundersBooks.com | RandomHouseBooks.com